An Inconvenient Mountie

Adventures of the First Woman Mountie. Book 1

LAURIE SCHRAMM

Front cover foreground image by the author. Front cover background image of Mount Assiniboine by Kurt Stegmüller, used under licence from Wikimedia Commons and Creative Commons. Back cover background image by the author.

AN INCONVENIENT MOUNTIE

This book is a work of historical fiction, set in the mid-1970s. Although most of the historical references are accurate, a few are not, and names, characters, places, and incidents are either the product of the author's imagination or are used fictitiously. Any resemblance to actual persons, living or dead is entirely coincidental.

Copyright © 2018 Laurier L. Schramm

All worldwide rights reserved, including those of translation into other languages. No part of this book may be reproduced in any form, electronic or mechanical, including by photo-printing, microfilm, or any other means, nor transmitted or translated into a machine language without written permission from the publisher. Please acquire only authorized editions. Registered names, trademarks, and the like, used in this book, even when not specifically marked or identified as such, are not to be considered unprotected by law.

Print ISBN: 978-1-9994940-0-1
ePub ISBN: 978-1-9994940-1-8

Laurie Schramm

AN INCONVENIENT MOUNTIE

```
M
0535 EST+
RCMP PR ALBERT
V
VIA WUI+
RCMP PR ALBERT

RCMP RADCITY
```
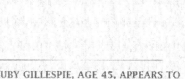
```
PRIORITY

FM:  RADIUM CITY DET.
TO:  PR ALBERT S/DIV
BT
UNCLAS
```
MISSING PERSON REPORTED BY RUBY GILLESPIE, AGE 45, APPEARS TO BE SINCERE. REPORTED MISSING IS NORMAN VINCENT POOLE, AGE 40, AKA NORM, RESIDENT OF RADIUM CITY. LAST SEEN R. CITY, ON 9 SEPT, AT 11 AM. INVESTIGATING.
ELS.
+
RCMP PR ALBERT

RCMP RADCITY
VVV

AN INCONVENIENT MOUNTIE

DEDICATION

To Ally.

CONTENTS

	List of Characters	iii
1	An Unexpected Meeting	1
2	A New Beginning	9
3	Radium City	17
4	Uranium Mines	33
5	More Challenges	41
6	The Bookstore	45
7	The Library	55
8	A First Lead	61
9	Investigating	67
10	Bell Island	75
11	A New Partner	87
12	The Guide is Found	95
13	The Trail Gets Warm	109
14	A Trap is Set	113
15	"Come into My Parlour"	121
16	Epilogue	127
17	Loose Ends	133
	About the Author	139
	Endnotes	141
	Adventures of the First Woman Mountie	143

ACKNOWLEDGMENTS

Many thanks to my editor, Victoria Schramm, and to my supportive readers, C/Supt. (Ret.) William Schramm (who also kindly allowed my main character to "borrow" his Regimental Number), Ann Marie, Victoria, Katherine, Moira, and Ernie for their comments and suggestions on drafts of this book.

AN INCONVENIENT MOUNTIE

LIST OF CHARACTERS
(IN ORDER OF APPEARANCE)

- Constable Alexandra (Alex) Houston, RCMP
- Norm Poole, Hunting and Fishing Guide
- Assistant Commissioner George MacLeod, RCMP 'Depot' Division, Regina
- Horace Best, Mayor, Radium City
- Sergeant Major R. Walsh, RCMP 'Depot' Division, Regina
- Fred Hoskins, a fellow recruit in RCMP training
- Corporal Mike Morrison, RCMP, Radium City Detachment
- Ruby Gillespie, Coffee Shop Owner/Manager, Radium City
- Jim Dumont, Hunting and Fishing Guide
- Dr. Evans, a physician
- Vern Schriver, a retired commercial airline pilot
- Jennifer Stone, part-time helper, RCMP, Radium City Detachment
- Lucy Weaver, Bookstore Owner, Radium City
- Ron McGee, a prospector
- Ally, a cat
- Jack McDonald, a fellow recruit in RCMP training, Regina
- Andrew Fielding, Bank Manager, Radium City
- Silver, an Alaskan Malamute
- Mervyn J. Crowe, a lawyer
- Franklin P. Heath, a lawyer

Laurie Schramm

Cst. Alexandra Houston

1 AN UNEXPECTED MEETING

"IT'S NOT HALLOWEEN IS IT?"

It was June 1975, and that was my greeting as I stepped off the de Havilland Twin Otter aircraft at the airport (more like a small airstrip, really) in Radium City, Saskatchewan. I knew what was coming next and as my inner voice reminded me to keep a straight face, I said: "No, not yet."

It was, in fact, only June but as I say, I knew what was coming next.

"If it isn't Halloween, then why are you dressed up like a Mountie?" asked the man who was helping unload the modest cargo of luggage, mail bags, and supplies for the town's store. He seemed both forceful and slightly sneaky in demeanour, a bit larger than average height and build, but slightly stooped in posture. I later discovered him to be a hunting and fishing guide named Norm Poole.

"It's because I really am a Mountie," I said, deciding to play it straight and wait for the inevitable response.

"Well, if you are, then you're the first I've ever heard of," said Norm. "What'll they think of next?"

I kept to my standard script, and simply said: "Yes, one of the first." In fact, I really was the first woman Mountie, but I didn't feel the need to tell him that. I hadn't even intended for it to happen at all. It came and found me.

***

There had been women police officers in Canada since about 1830 in Annapolis Royal, Nova Scotia, or 1912 in Vancouver or Edmonton, depending on who you listened to. I had always wanted to become a police officer of some kind, and I admit that I even harboured a secret admiration for the Mounties in the old classics my parents would wake me up to watch when they came on late night television. *Rose Marie*, with Jeanette MacDonald and Nelson Eddy, and *Susannah of the Mounties*, with Shirley Temple and Randolph Scott, inspired in me a fascination with the notion of becoming a police officer of some kind.

They say you should be careful what you wish for.

I did become a police officer of 'some kind.' Appointment of female police officers dated back to the beginning of the 20th century, it had only been in recent years that women officers had been allowed to become 'real' officers, as in allowed to carry guns and do 'real' policing – at least theoretically. In 1972 I had graduated from training and become a Constable in the Metropolitan Toronto Police force ('Metro'). My two years since then had mostly consisted of such critical policing tasks as desk-duty, matron-duty (searching female prisoners), and traffic-duty. Not that there's anything wrong with those jobs, they're important, and they need to be done well. But, for me, they didn't fit the Hollywood vision I had developed, and I wasn't finding them to be very challenging.

All of that changed with an unexpected meeting in 1974.

I had been called in by my Captain and ordered to go and see a Royal Canadian Mounted Police (RCMP) officer that wanted to meet me. My reaction to this was apprehension. I wondered what I had done wrong. I probanbly could have asked my Captain, but it was only my second year on the force, I was insecure in my position, and I was still a bit afraid of him. I knew how to take orders though, so I went to the meeting, which was arranged for a quiet downtown coffee shop.

Walking into the coffee shop, I was immediately waved to a corner table by an older man (these things are relative), with short greying hair, and wearing civilian clothes. I didn't recognize him but he obviously recognized me. He introduced himself as Assistant Commissioner George MacLeod and explained that he was the Commanding Officer (CO) of the RCMP's 'Depot' Division training centre and that he was an old friend of my Captain.

He'd already ordered a pot of coffee and launched straight into a volley of questions that ranged all over the map. He asked about my preferences for dealing with tense situations and volatile people, and I explained that I preferred to engage in discussions with people over brute force. He asked how I felt about Aboriginal people, immigrants, and visible minorities. I replied that I *thought any police force should be representative of the population that it serves, and related an experience I'd had patrolling in 'Chinatown' with a fellow Constable who was of Asian descent. I was just about to launch into a full-out discourse on the merits of diversity when he cut me off and jumped to his next question. With each question, he'd let me talk a bit and then cut me off and move to the next question. He asked about my girlhood, education, training in the Metro force, and my duties over the preceding two years. I eventually realized that I was being interviewed for something.*

Finally, he leaned back in his chair, looked at me broodingly, and got to the point. He had asked my Captain, his friend, to recommend one of his young officers for a special pilot project he had in mind. He wanted someone who wanted to accomplish things, someone eager and tenacious, someone chomping at the bit to be allowed to do some 'real' police work, and ... someone female. At this point, he shed his stern 'Mountie Look,' relaxed his entire body, chuckled, and said that my Captain had recommended the "biggest pain in the butt" in his Division - me.

Seeing my obvious confusion, he moved on. "The Force has fallen behind the times," he said, "it's becoming embarrassing, with political pressure for change mounting, but some of us have a genuine desire to catch up and build a more diverse police force."

"We're going to be recruiting immigrants, visible minorities, maybe even people with some kinds of disabilities as well, but we have to start somewhere, and that somewhere is by engaging women"

He went on to explain that as CO of the training centre he was ready to try a first "pilot test" with a woman, but that the pilot test had to succeed as it would pave the way for an entire first troop of policewomen that would follow[1]. *He had thought of using someone that had already qualified as a policewoman, and simply re-train them in the "RCMP way."*

That brought me up to full attention. "Wait a minute! Do basic training all over again?"

"Yes!" he replied, "that's the only way you can possibly succeed. In the old days of the Northwest Mounted Police, a person could get appointed straight into the Force, even as a commissioned officer, if they had the right political connections. No more. Now everyone starts out the same way, as a Constable, and by going through the same basic training. If you want to have any hope of being accepted, much less respected, that's how you have to begin."

"Will you do it?"

***

Radium City, Canada

Two years later, I'd arrived at the Radium City airport and played out the "IT'S NOT HALLOWEEN IS IT?" scene as part of my first introduction to a local resident, Norm.

As I collected my luggage, I was eagerly looking forward to doing some "real" police work. There was a large van serving as the airport shuttle for the four-mile trip into town, driven by – Norm, again. Although he had given me a hard time, the others taking the shuttle seemed nice enough.

Despite the name, Radium City is actually a town, not a city. It is located on the northern shore of Lake Athabasca, the 22nd largest lake in the world (8th largest in Canada), in the extreme northwestern corner of Saskatchewan, one of Canada's prairie provinces.

When we reached the centre of town, I took in a fairly typical small-town Canadian scene: a long main street accommodating most of the key stores and offices, with several back streets radiating out to each side. One block back from the main street was the RCMP Detachment, a standard one-and-a-half story brown building of the same architecture that characterized hundreds of small RCMP detachments across the country. That's where I headed.

When I arrived, I was greeted by a locked door with a typed notice taped to it, saying "Gone fishing. For emergencies, contact the Mayor's Office. Otherwise, leave a note." I noticed that the door also had a notebook and pen hanging from a string. I wrote: "Cst. A. Houston reporting. Just arrived. Will report back tomorrow am," and went off to check-in to the one hotel.

It was late afternoon by the time I had settled into the hotel, so I tried the Mayor's Office. I found the Mayor, Horace Best, was in and was eager to welcome me to the community. Horace was about average in height and build, with thick blond hair, and lively blue eyes. I found him to be instantly engaging. He would lean forward and look directly at me with a smile on his face and a twinkle in his eye. Obviously relishing the opportunity to speak to an eager listener, he soon launched into a sketch of Radium City's history.

I already knew some of the histories, having looked-up what I could in the City of Regina's library. I knew that Lake Athabasca was originally spelled "Athabaska," from a Cree word meaning "the place where there are reeds," referring to a reedy delta where the Athabasca River flows into the big lake. I also knew that Radium City had gone through a boom and bust cycle, and was now continuing to decline. Horace brought it all alive.

There had been mineral exploration activities in the area since the early 1900s, with prospectors looking for everything from iron, to gold, to radium. There hadn't been much development though, as the ore bodies discovered had been small, or the market timing was off, or both. Then, in the late 1940s, government interest in finding and stockpiling uranium for atomic weapons created an exploration rush in the region. By 1950, uranium prices had risen sharply, and prospectors' "tent cities" had begun to spring up around numerous mine sites in the area. By 1950, thousands of radioactive "surface showings" had been discovered. In response, the Saskatchewan government established the community of Radium City, in 1951, with the aim of serving the entire region.

Apparently, the city had been named after the "Radium Ore," everyone was prospecting for, this being the old term for the uranium mineral pitchblende. Horace chuckled, "The irony is that this radium ore was the same mineral prospectors had searched for in the 1920s and '30s, as an indicator of radium potential, but back then, the uranium itself was thought to be worthless and no one bothered to take much notice of it."

"Those were the days," he mused dreamily. In 1952, the government changed the regulations, making it more attractive for prospectors to explore and stake claims in the Lake Athabasca region. This even made it attractive for amateurs to prospect for uranium. The result was a massive uranium exploration and claim-staking rush that helped Canada build an international position as a uranium producer. "For a while, anyone with a rucksack and a Geiger Counter could become a prospector," Horace Explained, "and for a few years, the place was crawling with them." He showed me a scrapbook of newspaper and magazine clippings from publications like the New York Times, Maclean's, and Life Magazine, with headlines like *"Uranium - Canada Maintains Place in Frantic World Production Race."*

Several large uranium mines were established near the town, with the Rix Athabasca and Eldorado mines starting-up in 1953, followed by Cayzor Athabasca in 1954, Cinch Lake in 1955, Gunnar in 1955, and Lorado in 1956. With all this activity, Radium City grew from about 1,500 people in 1953 to nearly 5,000 by 1957. "They even made documentary movies[2] about us," Horace gushed, "like *The Birth of a Great Uranium Area* in 1953, and *The Road to Uranium* in 1957, and those movies were shown all over the world!"

"And the money flowed like water for a while," Horace concluded. Apparently, by 1960 the twelve mines and three mills operating in the Radium City area had produced about $300 million worth of uranium. This was big money in those days, and uranium was Canada's number one mineral export (ahead of aluminum, iron, and nickel).

"Of course, it had to end someday," Horace sighed, "We knew, or we should have known. But no one talked about it; no one wanted to think about it." By 1961, some of the mines had run out of ore and closed. By 1963 Canada, the U.S., and Great Britain had accumulated enough uranium, and they stopped buying.

"The next thing you know, uranium was a glut on the market, and the price collapsed." As the price collapsed, so did the exploration, mining, and milling activities, and the number of active mines shrunk to only two, the Eldorado and Gunnar mines.

"By 1964, Radium City population was 1,500 again, right back where we started, and it's still shrinking. Ten years later, and we're now down to about 1,000." To hear Horace tell it, Radium City was once a wild, frontier town, but that was in the past. With the boom and bust years well behind, it sounded like the town had eased into a nice, quiet life. There was a two-person RCMP Detachment, and Horace thought I'd find it nice and relaxing because, he said, "Nothing exciting happens around here anymore."

Horace was wrong.

RCMP 'Depot' Division, Regina

2 A NEW BEGINNING

"WHAT THE HELL ARE YOU DOING HERE?"
I had heard that before.

***

Having been sworn-in in Toronto, and given my permanent Regimental Number of 15425, I had travelled to the RCMP's training centre in Regina, which was called 'Depot' Division. It looked like a military base, with a big Canadian flag flying from a tall flagpole in the centre of a huge parade square that was decorated with monuments and old cannon, and surrounded by large, sprawling brown brick buildings.

Locating the Guardroom, I checked in – or tried to. The Constable on duty read the engagement card I had been given: "Houston, A., Reg.#15425."

"This is you?" he asked.

"This is me," I replied.

"But you're a girl!" he exclaimed.

Fearing that we were about to perform an Abbott and Costello skit, I quickly explained that I was a new pilot project of the CO's. This set him back a bit, but then he suddenly grinned conspiratorially and pointed down the hallway. "You'd better go see the Sergeant Major."

Reading the nameplates on the doors as I walked down the indicated hallway, I came to an old-looking, wood-framed door bearing a sign marked "Senior Training Officer, S/M R. Walsh," at the very end of the hall. My knock on the door was meet with a sharp, booming command, "Enter!"

Seated inside, behind a large government-issue wooden desk, was a square-jawed poster-image of a Hollywood-style Mountie. Expecting to repeat the dance that had begun with the duty Constable, I entered, handed the engagement card across his desk, and stood to attention. Without even looking at the card, he simply stared me up and down for a moment. "This is someone that doesn't miss much," I thought.

"So you're Houston are you?" he asked. Before I could answer he went on, "Heard about you from the CO. The CO wants to start diversifying the force, beginning with women, and then moving on to others, ..., visible minorities, immigrants, ... God alone knows what else, ... and DO YOU KNOW WHAT I THINK ABOUT IT?" He paused for a breath, but once again, before I could say anything, he went on, "I think it's about bloody time, that's what I think."

Sensing that there was more to come I remained silent.

"I see that you know how to stand to attention, and keep your mouth shut, so there may be some hope for you," he went on, in just slightly less than parade-ground volume. "I've read your file. I know that you're the CO's pilot project, and I know that you've come from the Metro Toronto Force, so you have some training."

"You're going to have to unlearn some of your training because we do things a bit differently in the Force (he said it like "IN THE FORCE"). He reiterated that he fully supported the idea of women becoming Mounties - "We need to be representative of the people we exist to serve" - but that I should expect no special treatment. He expected a high standard of work performance from everyone, in everything they do, and that in my case I'd quite likely have to do everything as well or better than the men.

You're assigned to 'M Troop.' The rest of your troop will be straggling in over the next few days, so you'll have time to get to know the base. Your troop will all be staying in 'B' Block, but we can't put you in there as we don't have separate facilities yet. There's an office with a bed next door to the Guardroom you came in through, and there's a bathroom with a shower across the hall from it that will be reserved for you. You'll eat in the Mess and do everything else with the rest of your troop." He then gave me a long list of places to go and people to see for uniforms, schedules, textbooks, and regulations.

"Come and see me anytime," he concluded, but "don't come crying to me saying something 'isn't fair,' because I'm going to agree with you – 'it isn't fair.' Deal with it!"

My initial impressions, having gotten somewhat over the shock of his parade-ground voice, were that he was probably highly intelligent, far more-broad minded than his outward appearance would suggest (playing a role *perhaps?), possibly fair, but tough - someone whose bark could actually be worse than his bite. I made a mental note to stay out of his "Bad Book."*

As my troop came together, and we started our busy schedule I found that my training for the Metro Toronto force had prepared me well for some things, but I wasn't prepared for how regimented things were, nor for the almost fanatical emphasis on neatness and physical fitness. For example, we ran everywhere. We even ran to our PT[3] and swimming classes, in troop formation, with the cadence called-out by our Right Marker[4] - all 32 of us dressed in the same T-shirts, shorts, socks, and shoes, and everyone carrying their bathing suit wrapped tightly inside a perfectly rolled white towel.

One difference was that the male recruits all got the brush cuts of the century. I wondered at first if the barbers had used an electric razor rather than scissors on them, and then learned that truth can be stranger than fiction – because that's exactly what had been used! They weren't sure what to do with me but settled on cutting my hair short enough that I could just barely tie it into a ponytail and push the end through the back of the baseball-type cap we sometimes wore, or up and inside of my forage cap. Anyway, we ran to the Mess, ran from the Mess, ran to class, ran from class, ran to Fatigues, ran from Fatigues.

Fatigues ...

"Fatigues" were named for the brown uniform pants and jackets that we wore while doing what on a farm would be called "chores." We had Fatigues every day, and we cleaned everything, our rooms, our building, other buildings, and of course, the stables. The term "Fatigues" came from the French word 'fatigue,' meaning 'duty that causes weariness.' They got that right! I was torn between judging that we were being put through all this to develop discipline and camaraderie, and my suspicion that they had an obsessive aversion to letting us have any idle time. I eventually concluded that it was both.

Hazing ...

There was the mild hazing all newcomers received. It was all very juvenile, mostly just silly, and not very much different from the hazing most students received in their first week of high school in those days. There was also the give and take of any new bunch of strangers that are thrown together in close, repeated proximity. Everyone was trying to get to know each other and look out for potential friends or threats. Naturally, there was an occasional incident that was more specific to gender. It would have been naive to expect otherwise.

One of our lecturers was a Corporal. I really don't remember his name anymore, or even what he was supposed to be lecturing to us about, which may say something about his abilities as an instructor. But, I do remember our first day in his classroom. As we were settling into our desks and getting our binders *out, he stalked into the room and took a look around at all the new recruits with a rather bemused, almost paternal expression on his face. That is, paternal until his gaze landed on me and he called out in yet another parade-ground voice: "WHAT THE HELL ARE YOU DOING HERE?"*

"I'm here to learn, Sir," I replied in a neutral tone.

"Name?" he barked. I supplied it. Checking his class list, he seemed surprised to find my name on it. "Well, Houston," he continued, "someone seems to have let a girl in here. There's a sewing class right down the hall, are you sure you wouldn't rather be there?"

I heard a few low chuckles from people seated behind me.

"No Sir, this is where I want to be, Sir."

"Hmmm" was his only response, and then he singled out the smallest person in the class and proceeded to embarrass and harass him. Being, for the moment, out of the spotlight, I felt uncharitably thankful for not also being the smallest person in our troop."

Most episodes, like this one with the Corporal, were pretty standard fare – everyone was singled out for verbal abuse from our instructors at one time or another, and to be fair our other instructors treated me just like any other recruit, no better, and no worse.

The most serious incident involved a fellow recruit. It happened one Sunday afternoon, when a troop-mate named Fred Hoskins and I were working in the stables[5], him brushing down a horse in its stall, and me mucking out an empty stall nearby. It was inevitable that our paths should cross, and on one such occurrence he reached over and grabbed my left buttock. This wasn't a casual, friendly touch like guys might hand out after a good volley in a racquetball game or a good play in a football game - this was a full-out grab.

I suppose that I should have handled it differently, but I was hot and tired. I was also probably feeling a bit cranky, as I'd been unsuccessfully trying to work out how cleaning the stables was going to make me a good policewoman. I'd also had just about enough of jokes and put-downs with regard to being a woman and having red hair, so without thinking I just swung around to my left and kneed him right dead-center in the crotch. I don't know which of us was more surprised, but it didn't last long as his eyes rolled up, his head and shoulders slumped forward, and he dropped to the floor like a sack of flour, unconscious.

Now what? It was Sunday, and there was no one else around in the stables, the rest of our troop having been assigned to a myriad of other duties. But, I had a wheelbarrow right there with me, so I pulled him up onto it and wheeled him over to the Post Hospital. I told the Hospital Steward that "one minute he was brushing the horse's tail, and the next minute he was lying on the ground," which was true but incomplete. These circumstances plus the location of Fred's obvious swelling led them to the obvious but incorrect conclusion that "the poor horse must have done it." Apparently, this kind of thing had actually happened to other recruits in the past. I didn't correct them about this one.

The incident was never spoken of again - not by Fred, not by me, not by anyone. On the other hand, it might have been my imagination, but over the next week or so there did seem to be a number of knowing glances, smiles, and the occasional reference to the legendary temper of red-heads. Nothing specific mind you, but it seemed that my colleagues approved. Perhaps it was all for the best, as no one else tried making a pass at me for the rest of my time at Depot. Fred later got into other troubles and either quit or was dropped from the program. I didn't ever hear which.

The only direct reference to the incident came when training was finally over and we were preparing for graduation. I was back in the Sergeant Major's office, meeting with him about something or other, and as I was starting to rise up from my chair to leave, he stopped me cold with his signature parade-ground voice: "Anything you want to tell me about young Hoskins and the horse?"

I sat back down, paused, looked directly at him, and in a firm, clear voice answered "No sir."

"Hmmm," he said, rubbing his chin. "Well, sometimes constables need to trust to their own initiative. Carry on."

My last meeting at Depot Division involved being called in to see the CO, Assistant Commissioner George MacLeod, whom I hadn't seen since our meeting in Toronto. He said he was pleased that I'd survived training, but that the real challenges lie ahead.

"Some of your colleagues want to get posted to the Musical Ride, or to a Traffic Section where they can wear big sunglasses and ride motorcycles, or to Ottawa to join the race for promotions," he said. "I don't want to wave you like a flag, and I certainly don't want you sent to a big city, or even to a large detachment - as you'll just end up being assigned to routine duties like you've already had in Toronto. I've recommended that you be transferred to one of our smaller, more remote detachments, preferably a "two-man" detachment. You won't be alone but you'll get a taste of doing everything yourself."

"Your colleagues will think you're being punished, but you're not," he added. "You want the full policing experience - a small remote detachment is the place to get it, and that's where you're going."

***

"WHAT THE HELL ARE YOU DOING HERE?"

Here we go again, I thought.

It was my second day in Radium City and as promised, I had presented myself at the Detachment Office promptly at 8 am. This time the door opened easily and I stepped into the office, where a Corporal sat sternly behind a ubiquitous large wooden desk. My orders said to report to the NCO IC[6], and this was he. He was alternately frowning at me and two papers held in his left hand. One was my note from yesterday and the other was a telex[7] form.

"Houston, A., Reg.#15425," he read. "what's the 'A' stand for?"

"Alexandra, Sir, ... Alex," I promptly replied. In training, we had been taught to look up to Corporals like gods. Angry gods, to be sure, but gods nonetheless.

Seeing that he was still scowling, I added, "Alexandra, Sir."

There was a pause, during which he looked back and forth between me and the papers in his hand as if he couldn't believe what was happening. Eventually, though, he crossed some kind of decision point and with a growling "Hrrumph," he dropped the papers to the desk, leaned back in his large wooden swivel chair, introduced himself as Cpl. Morrison and said, "Take a seat Houston."

For the next hour, he described the area for which we were responsible. It was not just Radium City, but a huge area of land bounded by the southern shore of Lake Athabasca, all the way to Camsell Portage to the east, Fond-du-Lac to the west, and the border with the Northwest Territories, which is 70 miles to the north. Less than two thousand people, but some of them widely scattered, and over a geographical area of nearly two thousand square miles.

From there he went on to summarize our duties, which comprised upholding not only federal laws but also provincial and municipal laws. As was common in Western Canada, the RCMP had been contracted to conduct provincial and municipal policing in this area. It made sense, really, as we had to be there anyway, and the cost of additional police to cover the other laws only made sense in heavily populated areas in central Canada and in big cities like Toronto, where I had started out.

Beyond that, as a small Detachment in a remote area, we were expected to assist our fellow citizens with a bewildering array of other things, from administering drivers' license exams to witnessing government and legal documents, to assisting with the delivery of babies when there was no one else around to help. He looked at me, and I waited for the predictable crack about me being at least suitable for helping to deliver babies. I could see the thought pass through his mind, as he looked at me with hooded eyes, but he surprised me by letting the thought go unspoken and instead talked about how it was vital that we quickly come together as a team.

He explained that there were only the two of us, with more work than two people could possibly handle, so we would have to learn to work together, help each other, and cover each other's backs. As he started to explain my essential duties, he increasingly lapsed into extolling the virtues of Allan.

Allan, it developed, was my predecessor, Cst. Allan Sharpe. Clearly, Allan had been a miracle worker. Allan had done this, Allan had done that, Allan had done ... everything. This Allan person was coming across like Dudley Doright (who was NOT one of my Hollywood Mountie heroes). *No wonder that 'Gone fishing' note had looked so well worn*, I thought to myself – with Allan here, who needed the Corporal? As Cpl. Morrison continued to extoll Allan's virtues, it seemed that my departed predecessor could do no wrong.

Contrary to popular belief, some police officers have a sense of humour. Trying to at least look attentive and keep a straight face, I was reminded of a satirical performance review that had circulated near the end of my training days. The highest performance-rating column was filled with assessments like:

"S*tronger than a locomotive,*
Faster than a speeding bullet,
Leaps tall buildings with a single bound,
Speaks with the angels,
Walks on water ..."

Finally running out of steam, Cpl. Morrison summarized Allan's exploits with a few more examples of how indispensable he had become. There was a pause, and then he looked back across the desk at me,

"... and now I have ... you."

With a huge sigh of resignation and the look of a martyr in his eye, he stroked his huge handlebar mustache and said, "We'll just have to make the best of it."

Seeing the look on my face (my jaw must have dropped a bit), he relented a bit and said, "Don't take it so hard Houston. Fortunately, nothing interesting ever happens around here."

Prophetic sounding words but, like Horace, he was wrong.

3 RADIUM CITY

My first task was to get my things and settle-in to the detachment. Our building had originally been built to house the larger police presence needed for a larger town, so there was quite a bit of extra space available. The upper half-floor containing three bedrooms and a large bathroom was vacant and unlikely to be filled up anytime soon, so I had the whole thing to myself.

The next few days, involved getting acquainted with the town and its people. My first stop was the Coffee Shop, which I quickly learned was the hub of the community. Having introduced myself to Ruby, the owner/manager, and settled in with a cup of coffee, I noticed that everyone seemed to drop by at one time or another. Some would come for a drink or a meal, of course, but many others came to cash cheques, use the pay telephone, watch the television that was mounted up high in a corner, purchase small incidentals, or – and this seemed to be the café's main function – gather to chat and gossip. As I later commented to Cpl. Morrison (first name still to be determined), the simplest way to get introduced to Radium City residents would be to just sit at Ruby's all day and wait for them all to pass by.

Norm Poole, to whom I had already been introduced as our aircraft baggage handler and airport shuttle driver, turned out to be something of a *Jack of all trades* who did odd jobs for other businesses in town as well.

Norman Poole

In one of the furthest corners of town, I was intrigued to encounter a ramshackle house on a huge lot that seemed to be home to several boats, none of which looked seaworthy, and a large pack of dogs of varying breeds. This was Norm's place.

It turned out that the dogs were sled dogs. There was an assortment of dog houses on one side of the property, each slightly different in appearance and seemingly built from salvaged lumber, and each having a flat roof that projected over the entrance. In this way, the projecting roof provided some shelter for the entrance, and the flat rooves provided places for the dogs to sit and survey the area. The dogs must have liked this arrangement, because most of them were lying down, lounging on the tops of their dog houses.

Although still a bit rough around the edges, Norm became more talkative when I showed interest in everything. The house, he explained proudly, came from four houses that he had dragged across the ice from the camp of a former Eldorado mine. He had essentially cut some of the walls away, butted-up the four houses together, and then connected everything to make one single house that was much more spacious on the outside than it had appeared from the exterior.

"Didn't cost me much more than the fuel for the truck to do the dragging," said Norm proudly. "I even scavenged the nails!"

The first thing I noticed on entering was the smell. Not the unwashed, hermit living-alone smell that you're probably imagining, although there was that too. The strongest smell reminded me of the section in most northern general stores where hand-made fur and leather goods were displayed. It turned out that Norm was also a trapper and amateur taxidermist. The unique smell of his house came from the odour of tanning fluids mixed with whatever he used in his taxidermy.

Norm explained that he was of Métis descent and that he had learned to trap, and its grounding in traditional knowledge, from his father and grandfather. He had learned taxidermy from an uncle who lived in Prince Albert and had a taxidermy business and display store there.

Seemingly, every room in the house displayed realistically posed, stuffed creatures. It was as if Norm had an entire family of forest creatures, all frozen in an instant of time while they had been going about their normal lives in the wild. I commented that I was used to seeing the occasional stuffed animal head on a wall.

"Sport hunters!" scoffed Norm, who warmed-up considerably as my interest in these became apparent. "Some people just want trophies to display," he said, "and I give them what they want – it helps pay the bills."

He explained that he ran trap-lines in the winter, and sold the pelts to the local general store. "Some animals, I keep for myself though," he said, as I was admiring a stuffed Marten that had arched-up on its hind legs and was looking ahead with its eyes bright and it's forepaws at the ready. It was mounted on a stand together with small shrubs and bunches of grasses. It had been made so realistically that you could imagine it was almost alive. All of his other household animals were similarly mounted, in lifelike poses, framed with several bits of realistic branches and flora. Norm had stories for each such animal, that were grounded in aboriginal traditional knowledge, respect for *"Mother Earth,"* and historical stories from his ancestors. Between the lifelike animals, their realistic mountings, and his stories about them, I found myself captivated. I began to perceive that there were hidden depths to Norm's rough exterior.

Norm was also full of other surprises. It developed that he was a hunting and fishing guide in the spring through fall seasons, which partly explained his yard full of semi-derelict boats – although he was quick to reassure me that his work-boat was very capable and safe. I later learned that, like many others in this remote community, he might "walk a mile to save a penny" in most things, but he spared no expense when it came to his boat and his truck.

Between his collections and his many careers my "few minutes to get acquainted" turned into an entire morning – a pattern that would recur as I introduced myself to other inhabitants of the town.

Driving down to the town's marina, I tried wandering around there. I was again surprised at the size of things but realized that, like much of the town's infrastructure, it had evolved to meet the needs of a community that was nearly four times larger than its current population.

At one of the jetties, another of the local hunting and fishing guides, Jim Dumont seemed happy to get an excuse to stop working on his boat and talk. If his profession was similar to Norm's, his manner certainly was not. I found Jim to be extremely outgoing and friendly by nature, and almost always with a smile on his face. As we chatted, it became obvious that he loved to talk, and was an inveterate storyteller – or perhaps I should say - anecdote teller. Thus, I quickly learned that Jim also had deep roots in the area, and was a fountain of knowledge about Radium City, its people, and the surrounding area.

It occurred to me that I could learn a lot from Jim, and as I turned to continue on with my explorations, I mentioned that I'd like to hear more of his stories sometime. I was brought up short by his immediate rejoinder of "It'll cost you!"

Jim was pretty perceptive. Immediately noticing the early warning signs of a bristle on my part, he quickly added, "A cup of coffee I mean. It'll cost you a cup of coffee."

Relaxing, I laughed, "Sounds like a good deal to me. You're on!" Although always ready with a joke of some kind, I would learn in time that Jim had an obsession with money, and did virtually nothing for free.

> Any complex organization must have administrative machinery to function properly, and the Force is no exception. A detachment member's ability to perform administrative duties is equally as important to the successful operation of the Force as is a well founded knowledge of criminal investigation. Both these aspects of police work are dependent on one another.
>
> ATTRIBUTES. "RCMP CONSTABLES' MANUAL." OTTAWA

I found small-town police work to be quite different from my experiences with the Metro Toronto force. Not everything was different, of course. Like police officers everywhere, we rated police responses to the urgent summons as our highest priority, regardless of whether these were from a criminal or public safety nature. But other aspects were definitely different.

The work-load was heavier because there were only two of us to cover a wide geographical region. This meant that response times were longer than would be considered acceptable in a large city. Fortunately, as Cpl. Morrison had wryly pointed out, there was rarely any serious crime to contend with.

Nevertheless, the detachment would get its share of calls. Our citizens had the option of calling our detachment directly (during regular office hours) or else to a dispatcher in Prince Albert (during evenings and weekends). The nature of the responses would vary. Some calls need only a short, quick response, while others might need investigation. These latter would generate official files. A typical day could easily involve see-sawing back and forth between responding to a call, returning to the detachment, continuing work on an interrupted file investigation, responding to another call, and so on *ad infinitum*.

Many, almost most, of the calls would turn out to be matters that would not normally be considered to be proper "police business," but we would usually respond to these anyway, seeing it as a way to serve the community, and build good community relations. I say "we," but that's really just a nice way of saying "I," as Cpl. Morrison would normally send me out to make the responses. As the rookie in town, and Cpl. Morrison's only staff, I accepted this as the normal way of things.

In larger detachments, and certainly in the cities, the Force would have civilian employees serving as dispatchers, and part of their job would be to screen-out most of the "non-police business" calls. In our case, however, during regular office hours, we would take the calls. It was a blessing to have the Prince Albert dispatchers take such calls on evenings and weekends though, otherwise, we'd have never been able to sleep or even take a break. But we would still review the logged calls the next day and generally follow-up on them when we had time.

A good example of a non-police business call came in early one Tuesday morning. Cpl. Morrison took the call and decided to send me out to deal with it.

"I've got a 'live one' here for you Houston. Dr. Evans has been called out to help a pregnant woman who's broken a leg, or something. It must be Mrs. Smith, ... apparently, she's fallen into the river on the edge of town and gotten stuck in the mud. One of the local kids ran into town to report it. Doc Evans is on his way but he wants help."

Dr. Evans was our only town physician. I knew him to see him but we hadn't become acquainted yet. Taking our detachment's truck, I was able to easily find the river on the edge of town and then drive cautiously off-road along the riverbank to the location of the stuck woman, at just about the same time that Dr. Evans had done basically the same thing in his big, bright red Suburban SUV.

Introducing myself to Mrs. Smith, whom I also hadn't met before, Dr. Evans and I were able to extract her from where she'd become stuck in the mud between some large rocks. She'd been taking a short-cut across the river, lost her balance, and fallen and twisted her leg between the two large rocks. She hadn't been in danger of drowning but, between her twisted leg and being nearly nine months pregnant, she hadn't been able to rescue herself either.

Examining her *in situ*, Dr. Evans judged that her leg was more likely badly sprained than broken, but her water had broken, and contractions had begun. Between the two of us, we were able to free her from the mud and rocks and carry her to shore. After another quick examination, Dr. Evans decided that it was safe to move her to the hospital, so we loaded her into the back of his SUV and I escorted them to the hospital. As I say, not exactly police business, but a worthwhile public service response with a happy ending (she eventually delivered a pair of healthy twin girls; just over six pounds each).

Another category of calls was the civil but not criminal incidents. A few days after the pregnant Mrs. Smith incident, I was sent out to respond to a complaint from one of our downtown store-owners. Videocassette recorders, VCRs, had come onto the market spawning a rising business in rentals of both the VCR machines and the movie tapes. In this case, the owner was upset that a customer had returned a rented VCR machine that had been damaged. The customer was claiming that it had been an accident and was refusing to pay extra for the damage, while the owner argued that it was the customer's responsibility and wanted either extra payment or charges laid. Hearing them both out, it seemed to me that there was no reason to believe that the damage had been caused intentionally. I explained to both that this was really a civil matter rather than criminal, and that it was up to them, but that the customer might consider offering some compensation for the damage that was incurred while the VCR machine was in his care, and that the store owner should recognize that he hadn't made it clear to the customer what the consequences of damage to the machine would be. I further suggested to the store owner, who was new to renting as opposed to selling things, that he might consider taking the experience as a valuable lesson and seek legal advice on modifying his standard rental contract to make it more clear who was responsible for what, and perhaps consider demanding a damage deposit be placed by customers in advance of future rentals. This mediation approach, involving taking the heat out of the arguments, explaining the law, and suggesting possible solutions, turned out to be effective in this case. Neither party wanted to see the matter go to small claims court, which would have been expensive in time and travel (since they would have had to fly to Prince Albert for this), and they both readily accepted my suggested compromises.

Slightly more serious, but still minor incidents would include something like a store owner receiving a bad cheque. In a small town, where everyone (but me) knew each other the likelihood of outright fraud was extremely low, and such cases invariably turned out to be the result of customers simply not realizing that their bank account had insufficient funds when they wrote the cheque. In such cases, Cpl. Morrison correctly predicted that the appearance of a "Mountie," in uniform, appearing on their doorstep was sufficient to prompt such careless cheque-writers to make amends. Police officers acting as "collection agents" was certainly not something we were taught in basic training in either the Toronto force or the RCMP!

Moving up the seriousness scale, our principal areas of actual law enforcement activity were: the Motor Vehicle Act, and the Liquor Control Act. In the case of the Motor Vehicle Act, there wasn't a lot for us to do. Radium City had a main street and a grid of secondary streets and avenues, plus a number of roads radiating out of town, and one short stretch of highway. The highway was interesting in that it was an official Saskatchewan provincial highway, but its nominal length was only 25 miles, stretching in one direction from the town to a dead end near Beaverdam Lake, and in another direction from the town to Lake Athabasca. I say "nominal length," because at the Lake Athabasca end it matches up with a winter ice road that is plowed every year, and which connects to the community of Fond-du-Lac, and from there to other northeastern communities. Along its short, year-round distance, the highway passes by the abandoned community of Eldorado, and several branch roads connect to the airport, the marina, and to various nearby abandoned mine sites. Summing it all up, Cpl. Morrison had explained that there weren't many roads, there weren't many vehicles, parking was pretty much a free-for-all, and people in town were seldom in a big hurry to get anywhere, so there was little in the way of traffic violations to worry about.

"Even vehicular accidents are rare quite rare," he explained, and then after a pause, "at least multiple vehicle accidents are rare, single vehicle accidents are actually quite common."

"Common?" I asked, raising my eyebrows.

"Common when people have been drinking too much."

This brings me to the one area in which we did have

enforcement problems – liquor. It wasn't so much Liquor Control Act violations per se, although Cpl. Morrison was apparently engaged in a never-ending game of cat and mouse with the town bootlegger, Barney. For some reason, every small town in Canada seems to have a bootlegger (or more), and Radium City was apparently no exception. Although the government liquor store has closed up when the size of the town so dramatically shrunk years earlier, there was a bar in the town's hotel, and two of the restaurants were licenced, but apparently, there was still a demand for Barney the bootlegger's services as well.

In any case, the problems with liquor weren't so much illegal sales, but overconsumption leading to occasions of fighting, property damage, and impaired driving of seemingly anything that moved, including cars, trucks, snowmobiles, boats, and even bicycles!

This brings me to serious crime. According to Cpl. Morrison, there simply wasn't any. He expressed this in tones that suggested extreme regret. When he'd told me at our first meeting that "… nothing interesting ever happens around here," he was mostly referring to the virtual absence of serious crime. I could understand his disappointment. Not that any police officer likes to see crimes being committed, especially those involving harm to innocent people, an occupational hazard for us all was to view serious crime and the need for criminal investigation as the "Holy Grail" of "real" police work.

"Not for us, the systematic process of investigation that begins with an incident or public complaint, requires a thorough and wide-ranging investigation, the arrest, possibly following a dangerous pursuit, and culminating in an arrest and a court hearing," he would say, leaning back in his chair, with his hands and fingers steepled over his chest. "In a regular detachment, Members[8] are required to be constable-generalists and might have to manage as many as 30 or 40 open files[9] at the same time, requiring them to spend as much as 60% of their time on criminal investigative work … but not in Radium City."

I quickly discovered two more things about Cpl. Morrison: he strongly believed in the relatively new concept of community-based policing, and he had a very clear policy on how it should be carried out. The concept, of course, is that police visibility and the appearance of almost constant police presence is, by itself, believed to provide a deterrent to crime. Secondly, highly frequent and visible police patrols are, for obvious reasons, very highly regarded and vocally supported by business owners and resident alike, both of whom have a vested interest in feeling that their businesses, personal property, and community as a whole are being kept safe. Naturally, in a small town like ours, Cpl. Morrison felt that such frequent, visible, and almost continuous patrols were best carried out ... on foot.

"In the big cities," Cpl. Morrison would say, shifting smoothly into speech-giving mode, "roving patrols are looked-down upon by most officers as being essentially 'security work,' or simply 'waving the flag,' and therefore beneath the dignity of 'real' police officers. But in these small towns ...," he said, his voice rising to parade-square volume, "in these small towns, we need to be visible, our citizens see this as possibly the most important service that we can provide to them, and it is a duty we must take seriously."

I mentioned that he had a very clear policy on how this should be carried out, and he did. This was the province of the junior member of the detachment. In other words, ... me.

My next introduction unexpectedly led to an opportunity to get a physical sense of the size and beauty of our entire area of responsibility. On about my fifth day in Radium City, I had gone back to the airport and discovered that one of the old aircraft hangers was still being maintained, and was still in active use, housing a single-engine bush plane of some kind. I found our local pilot busy taking removable seats out of the back of this plane.

Vern Schriver turned out to be a very pleasant, but somewhat reserved, former pilot from one of the large American airlines. He explained that he had retired early from his airline job, and retired "way up here" to get away from his fast-paced, highly organized and regimented former life. He hadn't turned away from his passion for flying, however, he'd simply traded-in flying big, Boeing 727 tri-jet airliners for his own personal plane.

Not really knowing what I was talking about, I asked whether he'd become a bush pilot.

"Well, yes!" he laughed, "Bush flying means any kind of flying that's done in rugged and remote parts of northern Canada and Alaska, so anyone that flies up here is a "bush pilot."

Vern Schriver's de Havilland DHC-2 Beaver

Vern went on to explain that he didn't fly for a living anymore, although he would take on paying flights if and when it suited him, which included anything that was particularly interesting from a pilot's point of view. He said that he would fly to Fort McMurray once in a while, partly just to be able to fly, and partly to pick up groceries when the local barge was late or undergoing repairs, and that in such cases he'd often volunteer to pick up supplies for other townspeople as well.

"Isn't that a long way to go?" I asked.

"Well, our options for getting supplies in the summer and early fall are boat, barge, or plane. The barge is the most economical when it's running. It's a long haul in a small boat, and commercial air cargo rates are pretty high, so sometimes a small plane is the best option."

Then, realizing what I was thinking, he said: "You meant, why fly all the way to Alberta instead of simply flying south?"

I nodded.

"Ah Ha. Well the nearest city with big stores, good prices, and lots of selection, are Prince Albert to the south, and Fort

McMurray to the west. Depending on the route and weather, the flying time to Fort McMurray is a little over two hours; the time to Prince Albert is twice that."

"Wow, I guess we're further north than I realized."

"Right. It took me a while to get used to it too."

Vern didn't look the least bit like my conception of the stereotypical bush pilot. Rather than being tall and heavy-set, with a haggard, unshaved face, he was slender, medium-height, and clean-shaven, with piercing blue eyes. I mentioned that he'd initially seemed somewhat reserved, but that didn't last long. If the secret to getting people like Norman Poole and James Dumont to open-up was to ask about their boats, then asking about flying, or more specifically, his plane was the key to Vern Schriver. I asked about his plane.

"This here's what we call a "Beaver." It was designed and built by de Havilland Canada just after World War II. They wanted to keep building airplanes after the war but needed some civilian plane designs that people would buy, so they came up with some planes that could easily switch from wheels to floats, to skis. They liked naming their planes after animals and called the single-engine one the Beaver, and the twin-engine one the Otter. This one is a Beaver"

"And it was made just after World War II?"

"Not this one. Some were. The first one was built in 1947, and they kept on building them up until 1967. Hundreds of them are still flying."

"Isn't that dangerous?"

"Not if the airframe is still sound, and if they're properly maintained and regularly checked. This one was built in 1967, and has been almost completely rebuilt over the years, plus has had all of its electronic, communication, and navigation systems upgraded to modern standards."

"Wouldn't it be simpler to just buy a modern aircraft?" I asked, starting to get interested myself, now.

"Simpler, yes. Better, no. It's probably un-American of me to say this, but the Beaver is probably the best bush plane ever designed. It's rugged, powerful, pretty easy to fly, and can land and take-off again in really short distances, on land, water, snow, or ice. Up here, that's awfully hard to beat. That's why they've been used for so many things, *'The Workhorse of the North,'* as people say –

surveying, prospecting, hunting, aerial photography, passengers, mail, and supply services – you name it."

"What are you doing with the seats?" I asked.

"Well, as you can see from these big doors on the side, it's been built so that you can easily shift back and forth between cargo and passengers, and I'm right now pulling out the rear seats to shift it from passengers back to cargo. It's wide enough for a full-sized 44-gallon drum to be rolled-up inside, but I'm just getting ready for a supply trip to Fort McMurray tomorrow." Then, looking at me more closely, he said: "I take it you're not very familiar with the north."

"No," I laughed, "I'm a big-city girl from southern Ontario. Most of my life, I've lived in Ottawa and Toronto."

"Hmmm, so you don't really have a feeling for the country up here then," he mused. "Why don't you come along with me tomorrow, we can get my work done in Fort McMurray and I'll take a slightly different flight path each way so you can see some of the country from the air. I think you'll be surprised."

"Sounds fantastic," I said. Let me just check with my boss to make sure I can take the day off and I'll get back to you.

"Sure thing, just call for me at the commercial air service office and they'll get the message over to me."

Promising to do that right away, I headed back into town. I expected Cpl. Morrison to take a dim view of traipsing off sightseeing after only being on the job for five days, but he surprised me.

"Great idea," he said, "It will give you some perspective on the size of the territory we're responsible for and help you lock-in some of the local landmarks."

"And Vern?" I asked.

"You'll have a hard time finding a more skilled pilot or a more reliable person than Vern," he laughed, "and he's like a walking encyclopedia. If you keep your eyes and ears open you'll end the day feeling like you've been drinking from a fire hose."

The next day, I met Vern at the airport and we headed out in his Beaver. Since there were just the two of us, I was able to sit in the right-hand, co-pilot's seat, so I had an excellent view, and he offered me a set of headphones with a boom microphone so we were able to speak to each other over the roar of the engine.

On my original flight into Radium City, I had seen some of the rich mixtures of lakes, islands, rock, and forests, and I once again marvelled at just how huge Lake Athabasca seemed to be.

"It's like another Great Lake," I said, referring to the famous Great Lakes that bordered southern Ontario.

"Yes, it's not really as big," Vern said, "but it's going to feel like it in a moment as we fly across it."

Sure enough, as we turned south and flew straight across the lake there came a point where I could barely see the shore in either direction.

"Isn't Fort McMurray to the west?" I asked.

"Actually, it's almost exactly south-west of here. I like to cut across the lake first and get it behind us. When we reach the southern shore, we'll turn harder to the west than we need to because I want to show you something that you won't believe unless you see it for yourself."

He didn't elaborate, so I contented myself with looking at the broad expanse of the lake below us. Once again, it brought home how isolated we really were, as in the entire flight to Fort McMurray and back I didn't see a single boat out on the water.

Watching the southern shore, I noticed that it seemed to be a greyish-brown colour, rather than the greys and greens of rock and trees that I was used to seeing. Looking over, I saw Vern watching me and he nodded.

"Keep watching the shore," he said.

As we approached ever closer, my eyes widened. "Sand," I said.

"Not just sand. Lots of sand!" he said, "keep watching."

Like he said, not just sand, but rolling sand dunes that seemed to go on forever. Once we were over the sand I exclaimed, "It's like looking a desert. How could a desert be all the way up here?"

"Not exactly a desert in this climate," Vern corrected, "but these are the Athabasca Sand Dunes – they are the most northerly and active sand dunes in the world."

"Active?"

"Active, because they are constantly shifting and changing due to the winds, just like in Africa."

"Where did they come from?" I asked, and then I answered my own question. "They must have been left here by the glaciers after the last ice age, but what an unusual formation to have in Canada!"

"That's right," Vern said, "The way it was explained to me, is that when the glaciers pulled away, huge amounts of sand, and silt, and whatever were washed into the basin that became Lake Athabasca. Apparently, 8,000 years ago the water level in the lake was much higher, so what we're looking at used to be the sandy bottom of part of the lake. When the water level dropped, this part of the lake bottom was exposed and there we are. But look at the scale of it all - some of those sand dunes are a hundred feet high!"

"Does anything live there?"

"There's lots of water underneath the sand, fed by the lake, and I gather that the scientists have found some rare plants growing there. Between the rare plants and how unique this whole thing is, the government in Regina is talking about making it a protected area so it can be preserved[10]," he said.

The rest of the trip was fun, but seeing the lake and sand dunes up close were by far the highlights. On the return trip, I remembered my primary mission of getting a sense of the size and geography of the area for which we were responsible and I marvelled, not just at the size of it all, but of how natural and unspoiled it all was. As we approached Radium City I did, this time, spot a couple of small boats out on the lake, and the occasional cabin on a point of land or small island. I thanked Vern more than once for this eye-opening adventure and offered to pay for his fuel. He had graciously allowed me to buy him lunch in Fort McMurray but refused to take anything else, saying that it was nice to have had the company and fun showing me some of the sights.

Over the next few days, I got to know the town quite well and was ready to see more of the surrounding areas.

Laurie Schramm

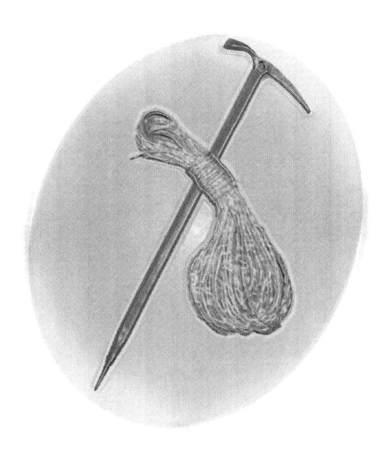

4 URANIUM MINES

I DON'T HAVE THE RIGHT EQUIPMENT FOR THIS!
I get *déjà vu* a lot.

* * *

It was 1972. I had been mountaineering with a cousin in the mountains near Jasper, Alberta. We had been hiking along a trail on a very steep slope, following a fairly clear game trail. The trail was probably one of many that were used daily by Mule Deer in the area. Then, suddenly, we lost the trail. All we could see was rock, long grasses, and some short trees. By itself, this was only inconvenient, as we could always retreat back the way we had come, except that we had noticed storm clouds working their way down the valley towards us.

When we had taken our mountaineering – rock climbing course the year before, our Mountain Guide/Instructor had warned of how quickly a storm could roll down the valley, and the danger from lightning if caught up high, especially on an exposed rock face. We were not terribly high up, nor on an absolutely sheer rock face, but we were high up enough, and exposed enough, to have become concerned. Now we need to get off such an exposed slope, and down to a lower elevation, and quickly. Retreating the way we had come was feasible but very time-consuming. Much better would be to simply descend directly down the slope from our existing position.

The problem was that the slope was too steep for us to walk or slide down without losing control and falling the rest of the way. Looking ahead, we noticed that there was a solid-looking tree not too far away that, when we got to it, exhibited bits of frayed nylon webbing lying at its base. This suggested that previous climbers had used the tree as an anchor point for rappelling down. The frayed pieces of webbing all looked too old and frayed to trust, and I remember thinking, "I don't have the right equipment for this!"

We had brought minimal climbing equipment with us because we had only planned to practice rock climbing on short faces, climbing one at a time, while the other belayed from above. We had climbing harnesses, a 50 m length of 9mm climbing rope, a couple of slings, an alloy Figure 8 self-belay device[11]*, and our gloves. We tied our two slings together so that they would reach around the tree leaving a loop hanging around each side, then fed our rope exactly half-way through both loops. Our 50 m rope was now only 25 m long. Allowing for the rope that had to be bent around the Figure-8, and a bit of a gap from the rock slope, that gave us about 80 feet of coverage. Looking down, the next level that seemed to have a bit of path or at least a lot of rocky protrusions looked like it* **might not** *be more than 80 feet down. It was hard to be sure.*

With the storm advancing rapidly, we decided to give it a try. We attached the Figure-8 to the rope and my harness, knotted the two free ends together to prevent inadvertently rappelling right off the ends of the rope, and threw the knotted end out and down the face. I started rappelling down. As I worked my way down, it was still hard to judge the conditions at the bottom of the rope, but it didn't look too bad. As I neared the end of the twinned rope, I found that I could securely stand on some rock protrusions, and as I looked around, I could see another game trail that seemed to angle downwards. Breathing a sigh of relief, I slipped the rope off the Figure-8. It was fortunate that I didn't lose my one-handed grip on the rope because as it came away from the Figure-8 there was a strong upwards pull. At first, I thought it was my cousin but then realized that it was the slight elastic stretch in the rope. Climbing ropes are designed to stretch a bit in order to absorb some of the shocks should a climber fall. Had it not been for the stretch in the rope I'm not sure that I would have been able to get my boots anchored and the rope off – a close call.

I'm not particularly religious, but I wondered for a moment whether to offer a prayer of thanks to St. Bernard of Montjoux, the patron saint of mountaineers, or possibly St. Simeon of Emesa, the patron saint of fools.

The rest was pretty easy. I tied the Figure-8 into the rope, called upwards "Off belay!" and my cousin pulled the rope up, retrieved the Figure-8, reset the rope and rappelled down. We reclaimed the rope and Figure-8 but had to leave our two slings behind on the tree up above, a sacrifice we were happy to make, and we followed the new game trail down the slope just as the lightning was beginning to flash and rain began to pour down.

* * *

> As in life generally, problems that cannot be solved by predetermined rules continually arise in police work. In addition, the nature of some situations demand immediate action ... the Constable who is confronted with such a situation ... must display a high degree of initiative and at times take a calculated risk.
>
> ATTRIBUTES. "RCMP CONSTABLES' MANUAL." OTTAWA

Cpl. Morrison had offered to drive me around some of the roads radiating outwards from Radium City. Other than the roads to the airstrip, marina, and a couple of isolated picnic- and boat launch sites, these seemed to comprise mostly roads to abandoned uranium mines. We didn't go to all of them, but occasionally we'd stop where a road would vanish into the rock, grasses, and scrub, and then get out and walk to an old mine.

In most cases, the only remaining evidence of a former mine would be some cement slabs in the ground (covering rises), or a cave-like entrance set into the side of a hill and covered by a rusty steel grate or some piled-up boulders. Here and there would be odd relics from the mines former lives: often just rusty bits of odd-shaped iron that looked like junk to me, but sometimes there would be ring-bolts in large rocks, broken heavy timbers with big nails or spikes sticking out, thick wire rope cables, and, of course, beer bottles. Every site we visited seemed to have its own unique scattering of old beer bottles. Judging from the shapes of the more-or-less unbroken ones they were of both recent and quite old origin, and I gathered that the roads leading to these old sites had provided people with convenient hiking, picnicking, and hunting trails.

Once we'd seen a couple of these old sites, I was beginning to detect a familiar pattern and Cpl. Morrison said, "Just one more, it's kind of unique." We drove along another road, that led to yet another hill. As the road suddenly turned into a path, we parked and walked a ways around the hill. After looking at yet another iron grate covered mine entrance, I looked quizzically at Cpl. Morrison, who only said, "Patience is a virtue." We had walked partly back along the path when the Corporal stopped and pointed out a slight depression in the pathway just ahead, that hadn't been as easy to discern when we had walked from the other direction.

Saying, "Wait here," he walked onto the centre of the depression, paused for effect, and then stamped his boot on the ground several times. Amazingly, each stamp of his boot produced a hollow-sounding echo. He explained that there were places where old underground mine workings went off in odd-seeming directions, as the miners had tried to follow the ore-bearing veins wherever they might lead. In some places, this led them to mine underneath roadways, pathways, and even ponds and rivers. Getting into the spirit of the thing, he then tried jumping up into the air and coming down, hard, with his two boots together. That was a mistake!

If there was a hollow sound this time, it was completely drowned out by the sound made by the ground and pathway immediately giving way beneath him. In a flash, he simply dropped straight down and out of sight.

I rushed-up, then slowed to a crawl realizing that more of the ground might be unstable enough to give way. Stretching my body out lengthwise, I peeked carefully over the edge and saw – nothing. Peering into the dark and the still-disturbed dust in the air, I called out "Are you OK?"

This was met with a moderately loud groan, and a growly "Yes, but be careful."

"Can you get out on your own?" I called down.

"I don't think so, I don't seem to be able to move my legs."

"OK," I responded, "Wait here. I'll be back in less than fifteen minutes." Running back to the police truck, which thankfully had the keys still in the ignition, I did a quick inventory. Standard equipment included a First Aid kit, a flashlight, a blanket, our VHF radio, and a body bag – I would need the first three, there was no one to call with the fourth, and I hoped not to need the fifth. The truck also had an electric winch on the front bumper, a long-handled shovel, a 30-foot tow-strap (for vehicle recoveries), plus electric jumper cables and tire chains (for use in the winter).

My first reaction was, *I DON'T HAVE THE RIGHT EQUIPMENT FOR THIS!* – but it would have to be enough until I could better assess the situation.

Starting the truck, I drove it carefully along the pathway. I had to drive slowly, and navigate around numerous rocks and exposed tree roots, but got to the cave-in in pretty good time. I parked the truck as close as I dared to the hole, then, having verified that Cpl. Morrison was still conscious and seemingly no worse off, I tied the tow-strap to the front bumper of the truck and eased the rest of it down the hole. "Can you see the tow-strap?" I called down.

"Yes, it reaches the bottom, I'm probably about 20 feet down and I'm lying in an old mine shaft so the floor seems stable."

Grabbing the First Aid kit and flashlight, shoving them inside my uniform shirt, I used the tow-strap like a climbing rope, except that with no belay device I had to rely on my hands on the rope and boots scraping along the wall, to guide my way down.

Cpl. Morison was lying where he had fallen. We had been taught First Aid as recruits, in both the Metro Toronto force and the RCMP, and I tried to remember our lessons. He was conscious and didn't seem concussed, but he was very pale and was lying at an unnatural angle. Clearly, shock was setting in. I asked about injuries and he said that everything felt OK except that he was woozy and couldn't move his legs. There was nothing obviously trapping his legs, so I tried gently exploring his lower limbs, then slightly moving one leg. Even a tiny leg movement produced an immediate gasp from him. I tried gently moving the other leg. This produced a louder gasp and his pallor went from pale to sheet-white.

"OK," I said, "Looks like you've broken some bones, one or both legs, and I'm a bit worried about your pelvis. Must have been the combination of the fall plus the rocks ... What do you think about waiting here while I drive back to town and round-up some help? I can try to find our doctor or at least one of our nurses."

Cpl. Morrison really didn't like the idea of being left behind. I really didn't like the idea of trying to move him myself and risk doing more harm. In the end, we sort of compromised. He ordered me flat-out to do whatever it took to get him out of that "Damn hole," and I agreed to give it a try, but insisted that I intended to disobey orders if it looked like I was going to cause more damage in the attempt.

So, using the tow-strap again for support, I climbed up out of the hole. It sounds easy but it was slow going, and when I reached the surface I was exhausted, and I'd had to rest a bit and catch my breath before collecting up the shovel, tire chains, and jumper cables. Using one of the jumper cables to tie them all into a bundle, as best I could, I attached the bundle to the hook on the wire rope from the electric winch and then used the winch to lower it down the hole. Then I tossed the blanket down and, for the second time, I used the tow-strap to climb back down myself.

I placed the long-handled shovel between his legs, explaining that I intended to use it as a splint, and then wrapped the blanket around the combination of both legs plus the shovel. Of course, to get the blanket under his legs I had to lift them slightly, producing more waves of pain. These waves were repeated as I started to wrap the first tire chain around the blanket.

Not knowing what else to say, and hoping to distract him, I said, "Now that we are working so closely together are you able to divulge your first name?"

"Mike," he growled. I knew he wasn't really growling at me, it was the pain, so I kept up some kind of feeble chatter as I continued to tie the remaining tire chains, in turn, around the bundle and then used the two jumper cables.

Standing up to stretch my back and view my handiwork with its bizarre accoutrements, in the soft glow of the flashlight, I started to chuckle.

"What?" growled Mike.

"Have you ever seen the old movie called *'The Mummy'* with Boris Karloff?"

He tried to laugh, but it was cut off with another spasm of pain.

"OK, I said, no more jokes. Let's both take a minute, and then I'm going to wrap the winch-rope under your armpits, climb back up, and winch you up. Are you OK with that?"

"Do it," was all he said.

"Here goes," I said. I removed my boots and began to pull off my uniform pants. As he stared in surprise, I said, "No jokes, and no leering – got it?" He just nodded as I wrapped my pants under his armpits from behind and then up and over his shoulders. Tying the smallest loop I could into the winch rope, I passed the free end along and under the pants, and then clipped it to the loop so that under stress it would not turn into a noose and choke him, or worse.

Then, having replaced my boots and provided another reminder about not joking or leering, I grabbed the tow-strap and climbed one last, paralyzing time, up and out of what I also now thought of as *that damn hole*.

Activating the winch, I wound-in the wire-rope in short bursts, to allow Mike to use his arms and hands to guide his body to the nearest wall, ... then again to get him up to a vertical position, ... and then once more to lift him up to the surface. At that point, I was able to offer an arm and hand of my own to help get him up and over the edge.

"Very nice, Alex, ... ," he said, and before I could decide whether he was referring to the winch-trip, or his ring-side view of my panty-clad bottom climbing up and out of the hole, he fainted.

It was just as well, I decided, as I unwound the winch-rope, recovered and restored my pants. Just as well because I next had to drag him over to the truck, and then up and into the box at the back. I left the makeshift splint on him and checked his breathing. Still OK, but he was still out cold. It occurred to me that I was developing a pattern of rendering men unconscious.

"Make haste slowly," my Mountain-Guide/Instructor used to say, and this pithy saying came back to me now as I tried to drive as quickly as I could without causing too much bouncing and jarring, all the way back to our town's small hospital.

Cpl. Mike Morrison

5 MORE CHALLENGES

We had a small, but pretty well set-up hospital in Radium City, with one doctor (the Dr. Evans I helped with the pregnant Mrs. Smith), two nurses, a few other staff, two examination rooms, an X-ray machine, multi-purpose surgery, and two six-bed wards.

Dr. Evans found broken bones in both legs and a fractured pelvis. He assured me that jury-splinting his legs and getting him in right away was the best thing I could have done in the circumstances and that while the bouncing around in the truck hadn't done his fractures any good, it was far preferable to the alternatives.

This left Cpl. Morrison (I had mentally reverted to our formal form of address) lying in bed, in traction, with both legs elevated and in casts. Dr. Evans explained that some of the bone had been torn away from the pelvis and that he couldn't be certain, but it could take as much as 6 weeks before he could graduate to limited mobility with crutches.

Correctly interpreting my slightly horrified expression, he relented a bit. "Maybe less could be four weeks, ... we'll have to see."

Learning that I wouldn't be able to talk to Cpl. Morrison until the next morning, I left for the Detachment to file a report.

Prince Albert Sub-Division, I thought, was going to love this.

An hour later, having sent a brief report by telex, I crawled into bed and fell instantly asleep. The next morning, there was a reply waiting for me in the teletype machine:

FM: PR ALBERT S/DIV
TO: RADIUM CITY DET.
BT
UNCLAS

UNFORTUNATE CPL. M. INJURED. NO REPLACEMENT AVAILABLE AT PRESENT. HOLD THE FORT.
ELS.

In other words: I was on my own until further notice.

My first stop was the hospital, but Cpl. Morrison was too heavily sedated to do much more than wave at me in dim recognition. Things were quiet in town, so I continued exploring and meeting the residents.

By the evening of his second day in the hospital, Cpl. Morrison was much more alert, and the two of us held Dr. Evans spellbound as we compared our recollections of the events and emotions of our recent wilderness experience. After an hour of this, and worried that I was tiring Cpl. Morrison out, I got up to take a tour around town and had made it partway through the door when his gruff "Constable Houston!" caught me in mid-stride. Turning, I straightened up and said, "Yes, Sir?"

"Permission granted to continue referring to me as 'Mike' ..."

Were the corners of his mouth turning up ever so slightly?

"Yes, Sss... Mike," I replied, and walked out feeling just a bit taller than when I had first arrived in Radium City.

As the days went by, we settled into a pattern of regular morning and evening visits.

To my surprise, his initially gruff and grudging acceptance of his fate in having been "saddled" with me had been completely replaced with the manner of a teacher, and then, sometime later, ... a coach.

Mike felt that we should get some local part-time help to cover the bulk of the non-policing, administrative tasks around the detachment like office reception, logging citizen queries and complaints, answering the phone, watching the teletype machine, and so on. To this end, he told me to send a telex to Prince Albert Sub-Division requesting permission to hire some local part-time help until either they were able to send a replacement, or else Mike was released for duty by Dr. Evans.

My experience on the Metro Toronto police force had left me with a low opinion of any big-system bureaucracy's willingness to spend unbudgeted money, but Mike simply said: "Give it a try." Sure enough, the next day the office teletype rattled away and the keys typed out a reply:

APPROVE HIRING LOCAL HELP FOR ADMIN DUTIES. MINIMIZE COST.

That, of course, meant find a great person that would work long hours and do a great job, for not much pay. Chuckling at my interpretation, Mike then suggested a few people in town that he thought might be willing, available, and suitable for this work, but he left it up to me to meet and interview them, make the decisions, and engage them under contract to the Force.

In the end, I hired Jennifer Stone, Ruby Gillespie's niece. Jennifer was nineteen years old, had just graduated from high school, and was trying to decide what to do next in life. While pondering this, she had been working part-time at the coffee shop, but Ruby really only needed her for the peak, lunch and dinner meal periods. This meant that, for most of the mornings and afternoons, Jennifer could watch over our phone and teletype machine, and handle walk-in inquiries. She was a quick study and a hard worker. Having mastered the phone and telex in a matter of minutes, she was eager for more and, wonder of wonders, she could type! A single demonstration proved that she could not only type, but faster than I could. I quickly sorted our piles of handwritten files and notes into two piles: confidential and non-confidential. Extracting a promise from her to stay out of the former, I turned her loose on the latter.

Meanwhile, my meetings with Mike settled into a pattern. He would explain what needed to be done, make a few suggestions to get me started, and then leave me to do the rest – try things, make decisions, succeed or fail, and report back. In the evenings, we'd discuss what, if anything, I'd learned from each and every new experience. His breadth and depth of knowledge and experience were formidable, but I think I was most impressed with how personally committed he obviously was to the job. It didn't seem possible, but he appeared to have both studied and built relationships with almost every one of our town's four hundred or so adults. I had expected that having spent some time in the community that he would know almost everyone "by sight," he seemed to know them all by name. Every time I related a fresh meeting with a resident, and my impressions, he would add his own perspectives and we would discuss them. I was never able to figure out how he managed to get to know so much about virtually everyone in town, seemingly without having expended much effort!

My own routine also settled into a pattern. On a typical day, I would go for a morning jog, have breakfast, do some cleaning up and maintenance around the detachment (fatigues), and spend the rest of the morning on administrative tasks, including the endless series of reports that always needed to be prepared, updated, and filed. After lunch, I would work on our active case files. When I needed a break, whether morning or afternoon, I would drive around a bit, following random routes around town and the surrounding areas. Following supper, I would do an early- or late-evening foot patrol around town.

Despite the tedium of some of the administrative work and the mundane nature of some of the calls, overall it was frightening, stretching, rewarding, exhausting, and fun – all at the same time. I think I learned more in the next three weeks than in any other three-week period of my life.

I suppose it couldn't have lasted forever. In week number four, things changed.

6 THE BOOKSTORE

I CAN'T BREATHE!

***

I've read that everyone has natural talents for some things. If so, the converse is probably true as well. Wrestling, for example, is not one of my talents.

In training, they had started us off with wrestling, as a prelude to self-defence training. I hadn't been good at wrestling when I trained for the Metro Toronto force, and I wasn't good at it in Depot Division training either.

They would demonstrate a move or two, then have us try it in turns. One day, when my turn came up, I'd been partnered with a recruit that was quite a bit larger, and heavier than I am. This didn't seem fair to me at the time, and I wondered whether it was a case of being mean or discriminatory on the part of my instructor. I'm glad that I didn't make an issue of it though because looking back on it, I realized that it was realistic, and good preparation for real-life situations that could come up later.

We hadn't jostled for grips and positioning very long before I found that my legs had been cut out from under me and I'd been driven face-down to the floor, ... and I mean well pinned, flat on the floor, with my arms and legs stretched straight out.

My wrestling partner was not only heavier, but stronger and more skilled, and I found that I couldn't break his holds, nor slither forwards, backward, or *to either side. Having tried all of these in turn, I was tiring quickly and finding it more and more difficult to get air into my lungs. I had just enough time for the left (logical/rational) side of my brain to think, "Great!" before the right (emotional/intuitive) side started sending an emergency "I can't breathe!" message that was impossible to ignore.*

What happened next came from instinct, not thought or planning.

I took a long slow breath, gritted my teeth, and eased slowly up onto my knees and put everything I had into my arms, back, and legs, to rise up on my forearms. My partner kept his holds in place and perfectly maintained his balance on top of me. He seemed inclined to simply wait for me to inevitably tire and drop back down again. Taking another deep breath, I again put everything I had into my arms, back, and legs, but this time focused all my energy on levering my back upright. I had under-estimated my strength, and rather than simply rising up, I snapped up so quickly that my partner was thrown up and off me. As he crashed down to the floor, I looked over, and I don't know who was the more surprised, him, me, or our instructor.

Our instructor said, "Unusual, but effective ... nice!" I seemed to have earned some approval from my troop-mates as well because as we later headed for our respective shower-rooms, there was a loud "Crack!," as the tip of an accurate towel-snap just made contact with my butt, followed by someone saying, sotto voce, "Nice job, Red."

Although I certainly have the hair for it, I've never liked being called "Red." In this case, however, I was relieved and pleased, rather than offended, and I gratefully accepted it all in the spirit with which it had been delivered.

***

Now I was experiencing the same thing all over again, this time in Radium City.

I had been doing my last walking patrol around the streets of the town. It was late, probably near midnight, and the cool night air contributed to an eerie atmosphere as I listened to the sound of my boots on the boardwalk. I tested the doorknobs of the shops as I walked along. They were all locked, but as I tested the door of the bookstore, I thought I detected something move in the grey darkness near the back of the store. Peripheral vision isn't always very reliable, but I decided to walk around the back of the store, just to be sure.

Having made my way down the next lane and around the back, sure enough, the back door was unlocked and slightly ajar. This wasn't a rare occurrence. Small town residents didn't usually lock the doors of their houses or even their vehicles for that matter. Shopkeepers were usually a bit more careful, however, for obvious reasons, but even they tended towards complacency, secure in the knowledge that "nothing ever happens around here."

As I went into the back of the store, my adrenalin was up a bit and I was careful to be quiet, but I wasn't overly concerned. I had just made my way through the back storeroom and was stepping into the main part of the store when I felt a huge weight on my back as someone jumped from somewhere above and behind me onto my back, pushing me forward and driving me face-down to the floor.

Whomever it was had the advantage of greater weight and must have had some experience wrestling, as I soon found that I was fully pinned down and could barely move. I couldn't effectively grab anything for leverage, and I was having trouble getting enough air into my lungs to be able to try much else. *Damn it all, it's happening again*, I thought, as I flashed back to my training days.

Sometimes you rely on your training, sometimes on your experiences.

In this case, the same old instinct from before kicked-in. I took a long slow breath. Just like in training, again, I eased slowly up onto my knees and put everything I had into my arms, back, and legs, to rise up on my forearms. My assailant stayed in place and seemed more intent on maintaining the *status quo* than on trying anything new. Having taken another long slow breath, I again put everything I had into my back and legs, and this time focused all my energy on using my back to lever myself straight up – as quickly as I possibly could. For a wonder, it worked again.

Like in training, I don't know which of us was more surprised, but my assailant was thrown up, backward and to my left side. As we went down, he kicked out, pushing me over to my right side and back down to the floor. This time, however, his mind was on flight, and he scrambled to his feet and immediately ran off towards the back of the store. He must have had some familiarity with the layout of the store's bookcases because he didn't waste any time getting out. I'm saying "he" because I had the impression that my assailant was male, although I wasn't sure.

Despite getting up as quickly as I could and launching out in pursuit, a combination of darkness and my own unfamiliarity with the store had me stumbling into chairs and bookcases. The result was that by the time I reached the back of the store and out into the back lane, there was nothing to see. Not hearing any telltale sounds, I chose to jog to the right, down the lane and out onto the nearest cross-street, but I was not able to see or hear anything useful. Thinking it would be futile, but not wanting to give up, I ran back the other way, checking the lane and into its cross-street, but with no better results.

It seemed pointless to search the streets any further, so I went back to the bookstore to see if I could learn anything about what the intruder might have been doing. Reaching the store and turning all the lights on, I looked around. Although I did not know my way around the store, the only thing that looked out of place was a pile of books lying in disarray near the aisle in which I had been jumped earlier.

Someone seemed to have pulled out nearly a shelf-full of books and left them scattered as if they had been flipping through them looking for something and then discarding them haphazardly afterward. There was a flashlight lying near the pile.

Everything in the pile seemed to have something to do with prospecting or early mine developments in the Radium City area. Three of the books were histories of the larger mines that had once operated nearby, Eldorado, Gunnar, and Lorado. Several other books contained collections of old prospecting stories, with references to small mines that had been developed, or not, in the past. Aside from some bundles of old maps, the rest seemed to be leather-bound daily journals that once belonged to prospectors looking for radioactivity. Flipping through the journals I found that some were basically illegible, some simply contained dates and cryptic notes about locations and plans, while a few contained quite detailed accounts of dates, places, plans, things they encountered, and their thoughts about it all. It wasn't obvious to me whether the prospectors had been looking for radium or uranium.

As I locked-up the store, several things ran through my mind:

1. Why covertly search a bookstore at night? Was it an attempt to maintain secrecy? I had clearly surprised the intruder in the act, otherwise, he surely would have replaced the books on the shelves.
2. Did the intruder know he had attacked a police officer or was he just trying not to be "caught in the act" by anyone?
3. What could possibly be so important about a bunch of old books about prospecting and early mine development? Was he trying to steal something, or was he trying to discover something?

It was late. Since the store didn't seem to be damaged, I decided not to bother the owner about it in the middle of the night.

The next morning, I met the bookstore's owner, Lucy Weaver. She reminded me of my high school librarian – middle-aged, willowy, with thin brown hair tied up in a rather severe bun. Another thing they had in common was a complete personality change from reserved and rather formal at first, to outgoing and excited when the conversation turned to the subject of books.

Lucy judged, with obvious relief, that nothing had been stolen. She was adamant that the old books and journals, that had obviously been searched, contained a treasure trove of important historical information, but not in monetary terms. She said that they'd languished on her shelves for many years as she patiently waited for just the right collector to show up and buy them – but even then, she didn't expect to get much money for them. Although she was quite firm in asserting that, "***Anyone*** would naturally find them highly interesting," she "really could not imagine why anyone would want to do so in secret, especially when the whole lot could have simply been purchased for less than $50." I asked her to consider locking the rifled materials away in a safe place for now.

As I walked out, I wondered what it was about a bunch of mine histories or prospectors' journals that could be so important and require such secrecy that someone was willing to break-and-enter, and possibly steal. If it was something on the maps, they could have simply been purchased. In fact, they could have simply bought everything for such a low price.

That evening I related to Mike my experiences of the previous night and my meeting with Lucy. Mike also thought that the whole thing was very strange, but his main advice was to stay vigilant. I thought that was pretty funny, considering that three weeks of policing the town solo still had me looking over my shoulder and jumping at shadows at the best of times. Mike also had a specific suggestion, which was that I have a chat with "Prospector McGee."

The next morning, I headed out to meet Ron McGee, who lived outside of town on the edge of Nero Lake. I'd started out driving on a fairly rough, paved road, that was officially one of the province's secondary highways. After about half an hour, the rough road became a gravel road, and then something more like sand. Continuing along, I passed a number of derelict buildings that clearly represented yet another old mine site, although this one obviously had a complete processing facility, or mill, associated with it. I realized then that I must be driving on the old mine tailings, which I could see extended from the mill buildings all the way down to the lake shore.

Who would build a provincial highway across old mine tailings? I wondered. It occurred to me to wonder whether this had been a uranium mine and whether I was driving on radioactive tailings.

Eventually, I came to a fork in the road and turned left, towards the lake. A short distance down the lane I came to a large log cabin that looked like a Hollywood image of an old trapper's cabin. It looked very old, was sagging a bit in a few places, and even had old-style wooden snowshoes and a rack of deer antlers hung-up on the outer walls.

The resident had obviously heard the sound of my truck approaching because I no sooner turned off the engine than the front door opened and a wizened old man came out to see who I was. He certainly looked like a prospector to me, with greying, longish hair, and the grizzled look that comes from not having shaved for a week or so. He peered out at me with penetrating eyes and bushy eyebrows. His eyebrows reminded me of Mike's.

I identified myself as a police officer and asked if I could come in and ask him a few questions related to an investigation that I was conducting.

He was quite taken with the fact that I was a woman Mountie. "But you're a girl!" was his first statement.

Sigh.

I explained the whole being a woman thing, and he took a moment to get it all clear in his mind.

"Well, isn't that the durndest thing? ... Whatever will they think up next?" he exclaimed.

These seemed like rhetorical questions, so I moved on to explain that I was investigating a mysterious break-in that had happened in town, that it seemed to have something to do with old mines and prospecting, and that my boss had suggested that he might be able to help me.

Seeming satisfied, he introduced himself as Ron McGee and confirmed that he was a part-time prospector. When I mentioned that his home looked more like a trapper's cabin than a prospector's, he chuckled.

"I'm also a part-time trapper," he explained in a deep Scottish accent. Then, with a sly expression, he confided that he wasn't a very good trapper, but that under an old provincial law, trappers of Aboriginal heritage were allowed to live on government-owned land in order to pursue trapping on traditional hunting grounds.

"I'm only allowed to live here temporarily, and only as long as I spend some of my time trapping around here, but it's free and that's tough to beat don't you think?"

Starting to get the joke, I asked him how long he'd been living there.

He'd originally worked as a conductor for CP Rail, travelling all across Canada, he said, but had retired from that after 35 years of "riding the rails." Now he just wanted to be away from cities and their crowds and had moved to Radium City to "get away from it all."

"I've been here for five years now," he said, "and I'll continue on here until the day I die, but that's only living temporarily – isn't it?"

Laughing, I agreed that life was temporary. I asked him about the highway and the old mine and mill site that I'd come across.

"That's the old Lorado mine," he explained. "It was one of the larger uranium mines around here during the Cold War, but it closed-up in 1960 and it's been abandoned ever since. The highway was built to connect the town to the mine and mill, but a lot of it's covered in tailings now."

"Are the tailings radioactive, then?" I asked.

"Sure they are!" Ron exclaimed, "but the radiation level isn't very high." Then, seeing my frown, he added, "but you don't have to worry as long as you don't live on them full-time like I do."

I wasn't sure whether he was entirely serious, but I let it go and asked how many other people lived in the area.

"Just me," he said.

"You mean the province maintains the whole road out here just for you?" I asked, incredulously.

"Well, I sure don't think they do a very good job of maintaining the highway. You saw how rough it is coming out here. But, yeah, I imagine they'll have to keep the road open as long as I'm still alive – and I intend on living another forty years out here!"

Mentally placing him at about sixty, I didn't doubt him. Although he moved slowly, and with his shoulders hunched over a bit, he reminded me of a Mountain Goat and I suspected that when he was out prospecting he could probably out-hike me without breaking into a sweat.

Ron explained that he liked his solitude and didn't have much interest in people. I found him easy to talk to, however, and he actually warmed up when he introduced me to his cat, Ally. Ally was a black and white American short-hair, and I would later discover that she and he were constant companions.

I didn't dwell on the cat, though, as I wanted to shift the conversation to old mines and prospecting. I told him about the break-in and what I'd found in the mess left behind in the bookstore.

Ron seemed surprised about the break-in but didn't see anything unusual in someone being interested in old mines. Ron himself prowled around the old mines, he said, looking for overlooked deposits of uranium. "There was such a frenzy in the 1950s that sometimes they overlooked things in their rush to find the big deposits," he explained. It was the small deposits that Ron was hunting for. These could still pay off for an independent prospector, he said, especially since uranium prices were a lot higher than they used to be "in the old days."

So, this was Ron McGee, our resident prospector. As I listened to his stories, it sounded like he was one of those people that were always searching around, without ever hitting "the big one." When I asked him about the specific materials that I'd found in disarray at the bookstore, he said that he'd seen them, or some of them at least. He thought the histories and journals were really interesting, being something of a prospector himself. He'd flipped through many of them, he said, but hadn't bought any because Lucy was asking too much money for them.

Driving back to town, having thanked him for his time and taking my leave, I thought about our conversation and judged that he was a likely suspect, given his interest and lack of willingness to pay for the books and journals.

The next day was relatively uneventful. Jennifer was rapidly devouring our backlog of non-confidential typing, and I was trying to figure out how to get her at the confidential pile. News of the bookstore break-in travelled throughout the town rapidly, of course, and by mid-day, I doubt there were many people in town that had not heard something about it. The general reaction was one of surprise that anyone would break into what one coffee shop inhabitant referred to as *"that dusty old place."* Probably the most excited was Jennifer, who was practically sitting on the edge of her chair at the detachment, poised and ready to note down any news or confessions that might come in. Unfortunately for both of us, none of the local chatter prompted any useful tips or leads.

There was, however, some excitement the third day after the break-in.

Laurie Schramm

7 THE LIBRARY

Evening foot patrols. Once our troop had gotten its bearings and settled into our training routine at Depot Division, we started to be assigned security shifts around the training centre.
The "base," was actually quite large. In addition to all of the residence, dining, and lecture facilities, there were many other buildings. One housed an indoor pool, a large gymnasium, and an indoor shooting range in the basement. The drill hall was massive, as was the stables building, which had a large indoor riding arena in its centre, and of course, several large fields for riding and for growing the hay to feed the horses. The base was also home to the administration building for "F" Division, which was concerned with the policing of the province of Saskatchewan, and right in front of that building was a military-style parade ground, beyond which was "The Square."
The Square was an approximately square plot of grass, with a tall flagpole in the centre, ancient field cannons in the two corners adjacent to the parade ground. The Square was surrounded by houses for officers and their families on two sides, and buildings on the remaining fourth side. Among these buildings were a large forensic laboratory building, and a restored, small-town style chapel. There were several other blocks of houses and buildings, but these are the highlights. The whole thing covered a substantial area.
One of the security rotations involved guard duty at one of the three main entrances, but I often seemed to draw foot patrol, which involved an evening walking patrol of the main buildings, the main streets, the square, and the perimeter of the occupied area.
One night, having completed most of my round, I was patrolling the perimeter and was walking along the portion that bordered the top of the bank

of Wascana Creek when I heard a muffled sound, followed by a series of 'thumps,' coming from the bushes on the side of the bank. My first thought was that it was an animal in the bushes.

Slowing my pace, I changed my grip on my large flashlight so that I had a finger on the light switch and a grip that would enable me to use the flashlight like a baton for defence, if necessary. As I got closer, I heard more muffled sounds – human. Although I couldn't make out the words, there were two distinctly different voices.

In my own best imitation of a parade ground voice I said "Come on out!" and simultaneously turned on my flashlight. There framed in the bushes, about a foot off the ground, were two faces looking up at me. The faces looked surprised, their eyes squinting in the unexpected light shining on them, and they looked embarrassed rather than threatening.

"You're going to have to come out, I'm afraid," I explained, "You can't stay here on this property."

As they came out I realized, with a shock, that they had good reason to be embarrassed. Jack McDonald was a colleague from my troop, and was mostly dressed – he was pulling his shirt back on and holding a jacket, which had apparently served as a makeshift groundsheet. She had very little on and was mostly using the clothes she was clutching as a shield, in a fairly unsuccessful attempt at preserving a little modesty. I recognized her as the daughter of our Sergeant Major.

"Holy Smokes!" I exclaimed, "If Sergeant Major Walsh finds out about this we'll have a homicide in our training class!"

If possible, this made both Jack and the young woman look even more sheepish. It was hard to tell by flashlight, but it seemed like the mention of Sergeant Major Walsh's name had made Jack turn a bit green.

As my mind reeled with the implications of what was standing before me, in my outside voice, I said, "Look, you really can't be here, but I'll tell you what. I'm going to continue my patrol until I get to the houses on The Square, and then turn back. If, when I get back here there's nothing to see, then there's nothing I need to report. OK?"

They both silently nodded, heads bowed, and I moved on. When I got to the houses on The Square, I didn't turn back. There was no need. If the Sergeant Major found out about this I wasn't sure who would be in the most trouble, Jack, or his daughter. As far as I was concerned, they were both old enough, they just needed to find a better place for their romancing than anywhere along my patrol route.

When Jack sought me out to thank me on the next day, I asked him how in the world he found the time to meet her, and advance to that stage! In the *middle of our non-stop training, exercise, fatigues, and odd-jobs, I certainly had neither the time nor the energy for such things.* He just smiled, looked down at the floor, and said, *"Well, you know how it is."* I most certainly did not, but I let it go at that.

***

I did evening foot patrols in Radium City as well.

Although I'd learned to respect Mike's police knowledge and experience, he wasn't the most energetic or active person I'd ever met. I already mentioned that he'd basically ordered me to conduct frequent, random patrols around town, and either that fact that I'd diligently followed-up on this or else the fact that I preferred walking patrols to driving, seemed to amuse him for some reason. I harboured a strong suspicion that he mostly viewed walking patrols as being too much work.

"A good officer has to conserve their energy," he would say, followed by his usual "nothing ever happens around here anyway."

If he seemed amused by my foot patrols, he was also serious about the need. I have to admit that I quite enjoyed my foot patrols. They got me out in the fresh air, it was good exercise, and I actually enjoyed the relative autonomy of being somewhat out and on my own. Although I conducted these patrols at different times of day, my preference was to go out in the evenings, when things were otherwise usually fairly quiet. As I walked around the town, I would check windows and doors, keep a weather-eye on vacant properties, and so on.

Apparently, the townspeople weren't used to such diligent patrols, because two nights after the bookstore incident there was another.

It was the library this time. I had chosen a rambling route for my evening patrol and was walking along a side street looking around and testing doors to make sure they were locked. The town library was a single-story building about the size of the bookstore. When I tested the front door, it was secure but my rattling of the latch prompted a muffled exclamation from inside, followed by a series of 'thumps.' *Déjà vu* again – the exclamation and thumps reminded me of the sounds I had heard that night as a recruit on patrol. That made me think of something human as the cause of the first noise, although the latter sounds made me think of something hitting the floor. This time, however, I doubted that I was going to encounter an interrupted romance.

Just like with the bookstore break-in, I ran around to the back of the building and found that the back door of the library had been forced open and was slightly ajar. Turning my flashlight on and drawing my revolver, I crept slowly inside.

Unfortunately, Murphy's Law was in full force. Now that I was moving extremely cautiously, fully alert with all senses on high alert, armed, and with a light, my measured investigation of the library found ... nothing. As I looked down each aisle of bookcases and made my way to the front door, I failed to encounter anyone. The front door was now standing wide open and proceeding through it and into the centre of the street, there was nothing to see or hear in any direction.

The Radium City Library

Re-entering the library, I turned on all the lights and proceeded to search for clues. This turned out to be easy. Once again, I found a pile of books scattered on the floor beside one of the bookcases. This was clearly the source of the sounds I had heard from the front door.

Looking through the pile, I found Geological Survey of Canada publications, with names like *Geology of Lake Athabasca Region* (1949), exploration reports like "Preliminary Report - Radiumfields and Martin Lake Area" (1939), and maps, like "Radiumfields – Martin Lake Area Map" (1952). The mineral exploration reports seemed to have appendices full of assay results from core-drilling samples collected from various locations in the areas named.

As I closed up the library, securing the back door to the extent possible, it seemed to me that a pattern was beginning to emerge. The bookstore break-in seemed to involve prospecting and early uranium mine developments, while here at the library it was exploration geology and mineral assay reports. In both cases, mineral exploration maps seemed to have been of interest as well. Although there was some consistency in the targets of both break-ins, it was far from obvious why there should be such interest in old historical documents. Did someone think there was an undeveloped uranium deposit out there?

When I met with Mike at the hospital that night, I gave him my impressions of Radium City's major crime wave, comprising two break-ins within three days, two messy piles of books, nothing seeming to have been stolen, and only minor damage to the doors that had been forced. I would still have to check with the town's librarian to see if anything had been stolen, but for the moment it appeared unlikely. So … not much actual crime, and no motive, yet.

"Try talking all of this over with the bank manager," was Mike's suggestion this time.

"What on earth for?" I asked.

"Andrew actually knows quite a lot about minerals, and metals, and money," he said, "If you show him some of the things that were being searched, he might be able to think of some financial reasons why someone is going to all this trouble."

Andrew Fielding

8 A FIRST LEAD

The next morning, I borrowed the rifled books, journals, and maps from the bookstore, and also the scattered reports and maps from the library, and lugged my cardboard boxes of clues over to the bank, where I had made an appointment to see the manager.

I found Radium City's bank manager, Andrew Fielding, to be quite distinctive. He was very dapper in both dress and manner. Over time, I noticed that he always wore a suit, quite like the way I always wore a uniform on duty, except that Andrew was the only person in Radium City to wear a suit (and I suspected that few other residents even owned a suit).

Andrew explained that among his many duties as manager of the bank, were assessing and approving bank loans to mining companies and (sometimes) to prospectors. Mike must have known this, hence his advice for me to consult with Andrew.

Andrew summarized some of the area's history, much like Horace Best had related to me when I'd first arrived in Radium City.

"In the early 1900s," he said, "there was quite a lot of mineral exploration activity in the Beaverlodge area, mostly focused on base metals like iron and copper and precious metals like silver and gold. The Geological Survey of Canada had sent parties out to determine the mineral potential of the area in 1935, and they found a number of occurrences of gold and also of pitchblende, which is a uranium mineral. That same year, a pretty good quality gold deposit was discovered not too far from Bell Island, about ten miles from here. The ABC Mine went into production in 1938, and produced gold for four years before being abandoned in 1942."

Andrew explained that the pitchblende deposits remained something of an academic curiosity until the nuclear developments of World War II led to a national strategic interest in uranium and a revisiting of the Beaverlodge area. By the early 1950s, purely academic interest had given way to an all-out uranium exploration boom, with thousands of claims being staked in the Beaverlodge area, ranging from new 'finds' to restakings of old gold and base metal mines, including the former Bell Mine on Bell Island. As a result, several new uranium mines were opened. Some of the old gold mines were re-opened as uranium mines, while others had nothing more to offer and remained abandoned.

"OK," I said, "so what possible interest could anyone have in these old, abandoned mines after all these years?"

Andrew thought for a while, and then said, "Well, possibly in hopes of finding some overlooked uranium deposit in the area, but that seems unlikely given how carefully the area was scoured during the uranium rush. There could be interest in mining the tailings left over from the old mines, but that doesn't explain the break-ins because everyone knows where the old mines and their tailings ponds are – the mines are well documented and the some of the tailings ponds are so large you can easily spot them from an airplane ... and more to the point, anyone could just go buy a Geiger Counter and go survey the tailings themselves."

"Wouldn't that be expensive and require a lot of training?" I asked.

"Not in the least," Andrew replied, "used Geiger Counters can be bought pretty cheaply – even the old instruments from the 1950s can still do the job – and they are easy to use. You just turn them on and listen for the ticking noises. On normal ground you get a slow rate of ticking, and if you get near something worthwhile the counter goes crazy. If the counter goes crazy you grab a sample and get it assayed, and you can easily get it assayed without telling anyone where it came from. In this town, with prospectors still prowling around every summer, that would be considered quite normal."

"So, if it's not uranium then what?" I asked. "Would those old assay reports show anything else of interest?"

"Not likely," Andrew mused, "everyone was looking for uranium because of the Cold War and the chance to get rich. Prospecting booms are like that, someone finds something and the next thing you know everyone's running around searching for their own little piece to stake, in fact ..." he paused, lost in thought for a few more minutes, then 'whack,' he slapped both hands down on his desk. "Wait a minute, I have an idea!" he said reaching for the reports with the assay result appendices. After flipping through a couple of them, he reached for a pencil and paper and his calculator.

I had noticed his calculator when I sat down in his office. It was the most modern thing I'd yet seen in Radium City. I remembered using one of the first pocket electronic calculators near the end of my university days in 1971. At that time they were just simple 'adding-machines,' in that they could add, subtract, multiply, and divide. In contrast, Andrew's new one had scientific functions built in and was clearly quite powerful. Andrew started muttering to himself, as he entered data, calculated things and made notes on a pad of paper. Then, he got up, pulled a book from his bookcase and started leafing through it before going back to making more calculations and notes. I tried to sit patiently and not distract him, but his growing energy was becoming infectious. Finally, my patience was rewarded.

"Holy smokes!" he exclaimed, "I think someone's after gold!"

"Gold?" I asked, dubiously.

"Gold!" he repeated. Then, seeing my confused look, he said "Look, we had a couple of gold mines in the old days, like the ABC Mine I told you about earlier. Back then you had to have a high enough ore grade to be worth the time and money it would take to get the gold out. The ore grade for the ABC Mine was about 0.05 ounces per ton – doesn't sound like much does it? - but watch the math here: 0.05 ounces per ton times the 1.5 million tons of ore that they dug out between 1938 and 1942, gives us 75 thousand ounces of gold. At something like $400 dollars per ounce, that means the company earned revenues of about $30 million – not bad for a company in the days of World War II !"

"Sounds great," I said, "what's the catch?"

"Two catches, really. First, only a few deposits were ever found that had enough quantity of ore and a high enough grade to be worth mining. Secondly, following World War II, the price of gold dropped. By 1965 it had dropped to around $270 per ounce, and by the middle of 1970, it hit a 50-year low of $230 per ounce. Made headlines everywhere it did, in a bad way, of course, because that knocked the stuffing out of any gold mining around here I can tell you."

"If that's the case then why did you just get all excited about the thought of gold?" I asked.

"Ah," he smiled as he sat back in his chair, "because after that the price of gold started rising again. In 1971, it rose back up to $270 per ounce, then kept on rising to," as he consulted his notes, "over $500 an ounce in 1973, over $600 an ounce by 1973, and last year it rose to over $800 per ounce. The 'buzz' on the 'street' in Toronto is that in a few more years it will hit $1,000 an ounce for the first time in history[12]."

"And that means ..." I murmured.

> During a diamond drilling program in late 1954 and early 1955, hole #FH-25-36 intersected 0.11 oz/ton Au over 38 ft in quartzite and ferruginous quartzite.
>
> Additional samples from holes #FH-25-1 through -3, and -7 yielded spot values ranging from 0.06 to 0.65 oz/ton.

"It means that an ore grade that isn't economic at $200 to $300 per ounce might just be more than economic at $1,000 an ounce."

Andrew went back to the reports I'd shown him. "Look here, he said," handing over one of the opened reports.

"What am I looking at?" I asked.

"These are assay results for core samples drilled back in the 1950s on Bell Island. Look at the part I've marked in pencil."

"Where it says 'Au,' that's the chemical language for gold. What they are saying is that they've found zones where the gold assay is actually reasonably high. Some of the zones might be quite small, so the whole deposit might not have such a high grade on average, but suppose that the deposit has an average grade matching the lowest of the samples mentioned in this report. That would be 0.06 ounces per ton. Let's suppose that there are a million tons of such ore in the deposit, which would be quite small for a mine, then the total value would be $60 million if gold goes to $1,000 an ounce. That's twice what they got out of the old ABC gold mine, but mining costs are at least double what they used to be as well. Still, that could be a mine that's well worth developing."

"Gold," I repeated, mostly to myself. "So now we have a possible money angle in all of this. $60 million could be a lot of motive!"

Thanking Andrew for his financial detective work, I swore him to absolute secrecy about all of this, gathered up my boxes of borrowed materials, and took my leave. As I carried them back to the bookstore and library I thought about what I'd just learned.

Even if I was on track with the gold and old mine ideas, why would someone take the risks of breaking-and-entering, and why break into the library so soon after almost getting caught at the bookstore? Either my mystery searcher was really stupid, or maybe they were in a really big hurry for some reason. I remembered my meeting with Ron McGee and wondered if it could have been him. He was certainly the only person I'd met so far that had a clear interest in the kinds of books and journals that had been displaced.

I now had some vague leads on motive and a possible suspect, but still not much crime. I decided that if things remained otherwise quiet around town, I would continue to investigate this whole business, as much out of personal interest as professional.

Laurie Schramm

9 INVESTIGATING

> ... as the circumstances of each case will vary widely, it is not possible to draft a set of rules that would be adequate for every situation ... The constable must have patience, as haste will result in an incomplete and inconclusive investigation ... To overcome the danger of forming a preconceived opinion of the case, the constable should try to keep an open mind.
>
> INVESTIGATIONS. "RCMP CONSTABLES' MANUAL." OTTAWA

By now I had many questions but not much useful information. I was trying to keep an open mind, but not too open, as I couldn't possibly pursue every idea. The mining connection seemed like the one clue that warranted further investigation, the rifled journals, maps, and reports mostly focused on the North shore of Lake Athabasca, and my instincts were leaning towards some kind of gold angle. My mystery person had probably learned these same things but may or may not have arrived at specific locations.

I decided to have a look at some of the lakeshore uranium mines that had been mentioned in the bookstore/library materials. This wasn't going to be easy. By 1950, the uranium exploration boom had uncovered uranium occurrences in an area spanning about 200 square miles. These were mostly north of Lake Athabasca, but that's a huge lake, covering an area of over three thousand square miles, and having a northern coastline of nearly 200 miles. For many of the mines, I'd have to go by boat. I did, however, have a list of specific mine names that figured prominently in the bookstore/library materials. Some of them had impressive-sounding names, like Consolidated Athabasca Uranium Mines, some were rather cryptic, like ABC Mines, and still, others had clearly been named for their discoverers or developers. An example was the Bell Mine, which I learned had been named for the prospector that discovered it: Thomas Bell. I decided to start with one of the larger of the mines, Gunnar, which had not only been a mine and a mill but also had an entire townsite associated with it.

Ron McGee had mentioned an interest in the Gunnar Mine when I'd first met with him, so I asked if he'd take me with him the next time he went there "to prospect around." He seemed pleased at my interest, said he'd been thinking about going back there and offered to take me in a couple of days' time. When the time came up, we headed out in his rather small boat – Ron, his cat Ally, and myself.

I think I may have mentioned that Ron and his cat were close, but it was more than that, the two of them seemed to go everywhere together. The feeling must have been mutual because Ally seemed happy enough to go in the boat with us. Ron had even made a little life jacket for her, that seemed to involve sections cut-out from a human's life jacket and attached to a small dog harness of the kind that strapped around the chest and both front legs, leaving the neck and throat free. I wouldn't have expected Ally to put up with the indignity of wearing a bulky harness like that, but she did and without a fuss. Once on the boat, she curled up near Ron's seat in the stern and promptly went to sleep.

We went by boat because there was no road from Radium City to the Gunnar Mine site. Between the small size of Ron's boat and motor, and the mildly rough conditions on Lake Athabasca, it took us about an hour to get here. I could appreciate now why they'd built a town at Gunnar. The site was huge, it was a long way away from Radium City, and the only ways in and out were by air or water (or over the ice in winter-time).

As Ron had explained to me earlier, the Gunnar mine and mill were opened in 1955, and by 1956 it was considered to be the largest uranium producer in the world. It didn't last though, as the uranium ore quickly ran out and the mine was closed in 1964. This killed the Gunnar town-site too, of course, and whereas at one time it boasted over 850 residents, by 1964 it was a ghost town. When we set foot on the site, more than ten years later, everything but the people still seemed to be there. The mine structures, the mill buildings, the houses and apartment buildings, even the school, cafeteria, gymnasium, and a huge shopping centre – but they were all empty.

Over ten years of abandonment had caused some changes to the site. Things were showing signs of weathering and rust, open doors swung on their hinges, quite a lot of the windows had been smashed, and bushes and small trees were beginning to push their way up through the roadways.

It turned out that the site was not completely uninhabited, however. As Ron and I walked around the site (he with Ally tucked inside his jacket), we did encounter a team of exploration geologists that were working the area. They explained that their exploration work was actually some distance away, but that using the abandoned houses as a base of operations was much preferable to their usual mode of accommodations, which comprised tents. I asked Ron if he was worried about the competition, but he said "no," and that the big professional teams tended to be out searching for big deposits of gold.

In addition to the exploration team, there was one other hub of human activity at the mine site. A fish packing co-operative had been established in an old warehouse that was conveniently located next to the mine's old dock at the lakeshore. Every once in a while, a couple of small fishing boats would come in and drop off their loads of fish. Ron explained that the business was pretty marginal, but as a fishermen-owned co-op, and with government subsidies, they were able to make a living. It looked like a lot of hard work to me.

Leaving the warehouse and dock behind, we next walked past the old mine itself and up a small mountain formed from waste-rock that had come out of the mine. Ron explained that they'd separated the uranium ore that was worth processing, from the waste-rock, which was not. When we reached the top of the waste-rock pile (which seemed like a small mountain to me), he pulled a

Geiger-counter from his old army surplus rucksack and showed me how it worked.

I had heard of these but only seen them in the movies before this. A Geiger counter consists of a sensing tube that is attached by several feet of wire to an electronics box. The sensing tube has a window at one end so that any radiation coming its way can get in. Once inside the tube, the radiation strikes the molecules of a special gas, which immediately separate into positive ions and negative electrons. The electrons are attracted to a positively charged wire that runs down the center of the tube creating an electrical pulse. The pulse is measured with a meter in the electronics box, which also houses an amplifier and a small speaker. That way, each pulse can be heard as a distinct "click."

"Neat," I thought. Seeing a scientist use a Geiger counter in a movie had been one of the things that had inspired me to major in science in university. Now I was seeing one in actual use. For the most part, we could hear about one "click" per second, but once in a while, Ron would hold the sensing tube over a place where the counting rate seemed to double, at least. As the counter clicked away at one of these locations, Ron explained that it was sensing gamma radiation from uranium in the waste-rock, but that the level was not high enough for me to be concerned about safety - as long as we didn't start camping on the waste-rock for days at a time.

Ron said that he'd scoured the whole site, mine, mill, town, waste-rock piles, and tailings areas looking for any sign of a residual 'hot' area, or even possibly a missed vein of ore, but without success. I'd previously told Ron about the library break-in that had followed the bookstore break-in. This was my *segue* to ask him about the old mine histories and prospecting journals, and so on, and whether he thought they'd be of any use to someone looking for places to prospect.

"I suppose so," Ron said, after a moment's thought, "but everyone out here knows where the uranium finds were. Even accounting for the fact that uranium's worth more than it used to be, we all kind of know where to look. Besides, it's not like you need to be a geologist. Anyone with a Geiger-counter can just walk around wherever they like and it will tell them if there's anything radioactive nearby."

Ron didn't seem aware of the gold-in-uranium angle and

reminding myself that he was a suspect, I didn't bring it up.

Thinking it over on the boat ride back to Radium City, it seemed to me that Ron was knowledgeable enough to be capable of figuring out the possible gold angle, but he'd given no outward signs of being interested in anything but uranium (and his cat, who had accompanied us on our hike around the Gunnar site).

***

After my trip with Ron, I didn't feel like I was any further ahead. Remembering Norm and his guiding boat, I went to him next. Despite his initial rough manner, my interest in his hobbies had led to a rapid warming up on his part, and we frequently chatted in the café and casual street-side encounters. I had previously shown an appropriate interest in his work boat, and I found him more than willing to take me out.

Norm and I spent a very long day visiting what seemed like the most likely old mines, working our way along the shoreline in the area that seemed to be indicated by the break-in materials. Time after time, though, all we found were derelict old workings whose entrances were blocked with rock or covered with rusty old iron grates. Each site we visited displayed a unique collection of odd bits of bent iron and pipe, and assorted artifacts from their old mining days: an old boot, a broken shovel, some crushed barrels, an old dynamite case, and the like. The only signs I could find of more recent activities were beer bottles, cans, campfire remnants, and related debris that I associated with partiers, picnickers, and hunters having stopped by to rest, look around, and eat.

Inevitably, Norm grew curious at my interest in these mines. I didn't want to divulge too much (everyone is a suspect until demonstrated otherwise), but as we took a break before heading back to Radium City at the end of the day, I told him that I had reason to believe that someone might be looking into old mines in the area. I asked him if he knew of any way any of these old mines could be resurrected.

"That would sure be fine," he sighed. "Most people around here would like the good old days back, but these old mines died when the ore ran out, not because the uranium prices dropped."

"If it had been anything but uranium, there might be the chance that a good vein was missed here or there in the old days, and that with modern know-how someone could maybe find a new vein and restart an old mine. They've done that in the Yukon, with some of the old gold mines over there, and some people are talking about re-mining the tailings left over from the old mines - to get the gold that the original miners left behind. But, with uranium it's different. Uranium is pretty easy to detect with a Geiger Counter, and the uranium boom had so many fortune hunters swarming the hills around here that there's not much chance anything was missed."

"The tailings here aren't worth picking over either," he said. "We only had three mills built and there's too little uranium left in their tailings to be worth anyone's while to go after."

I asked him how he knew so much about uranium mines, and he explained that his father had worked at the old Bell Mine, which was one of the ones we had not had time to visit that day. Apparently, Norm's father had been a part owner of the original mine, long before it and a couple of other mines were bought-up by an investment consortium and renamed Consolidated Bell Mines.

"Dad left me his shares in the company," Norm said, "so if anyone was going to be interested in any chance of re-opening these old mines it would sure be me."

Out of the mouths of babes, I thought. Out loud, I said, "You mean people still own these old mines?"

"Sure they do, they're all owned by companies, and all the companies have shareholders. In some cases, the shares are still valuable because the companies have moved on to other mines in other parts of the country. In other cases, the companies are barely still alive and their share certificates aren't good for much more than wallpaper. Those are the kind I have."

Ah-ha, I thought to myself, so if someone had an idea how to resurrect one of these old mines, they might not want the owners to get wind of it until that someone could first get a piece of the action for themselves. That could be a reason for stealth, and maybe a reason for break-ins and who knows what else.

Watching my face as I took all this in and considered the implications, he shrewdly asked, "Are you sure you don't want to tell me more about what you're really looking for out here?"

"Not now," I replied, "maybe later though, once I learn a bit more."

"Just let me know," he said, "someday you might need my help."

He was right. Someday I would need Norm's help, but by then it would be too late.

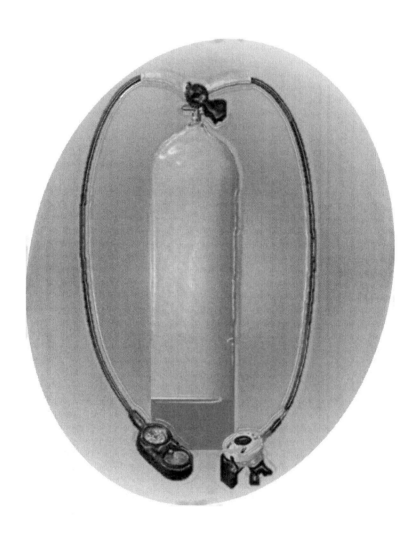

10 BELL ISLAND

"DON'T PANIC!"
When had I told myself that before?

* * *

It was 1970. I had been SCUBA diving with a university classmate in the St. Lawrence River, northeast of Québec City. We were exploring what was left of a ship that had grounded in a freshwater inlet so that freshwater and silt were constantly flowing into and mixing with the mostly seawater of the estuary. These conditions created turbid water and years' worth of silt deposited on the wreck. The ship lay at an angle following the sediment as it dropped downwards so that the tip of the bow was exposed at the surface, while the midship and stern sections lay broken at the bottom, at a depth of just over 40 feet. As we sculled around looking for artifacts, we hadn't noticed that our fins and hands were stirring up the fine-grained sediments, reducing visibility from limited to nearly zero. When I finally looked up and around, I couldn't see a thing. Not my buddy, not the wreck, not even my handheld less than a foot from my mask.

As I realized what must have happened, my first thought was: damn, a rookie mistake. As I tried to figure out where I and everything else were, my senses piled-on by becoming alive to the cold of the water, the hiss of the air coming from the second stage of my regulator into my mouthpiece, the bubbling of the air being expelled out the exhaust valves with my breath, and the air ... seemed to be getting harder to breathe. Was I running out of air too? Reaching around, I found my pressure gauge hose by feel and brought it up close to my mask, where I could just barely read the pressure at 300 psi. Damn, another rookie mistake. What had we been thinking not to have watched our air pressures more closely?

My SCUBA instructors had been "old school" type army and police sergeants. They put us through all kinds of elaborate practices designed to make us uncomfortable, if not panicky, in hopes of making us learn how to "deal with it." These exercises were usually peppered with friendly reminders that "panic kills," while pausing for a moment's thought can save. I hadn't taken them all that seriously at the time, but their advice came back to me now. I steadied my thoughts (and nerves). I realized only then that it was feeling hard to breathe because my J-valve, a mechanical reserve valve, had probably kicked-in and was trying to do its job of making it harder to breathe as a warning that my pressure was falling dangerously low. With this spark of recognition, I reached back for the metal rod that ran along the side of my air tank and pulled it sharply down, opening the bypass valve to allow a full flow of air to resume. What a relief! However, I had been warned, and I had little time left.

I needed to surface! I knew better than to try to just swim straight up because we had been searching under an overhanging part of the wreckage and I didn't want to get caught up in the dangling bits of twisted and torn metal of the ship's hull. On the other hand, I had zero visibility so I couldn't tell how to avoid the wreckage and get clear. I knew that I wasn't really deep, only around 25 feet to my position in the wreck. I probably had 4 to 5 minutes of air left, so I did the one thing the right side of my brain kept telling me not to do — I just hung on to a bit of the ship's deck and stayed still, hoping that the sediment would settle out enough for me to see my way clear of the wreck.

I lost all track of time as I focused alternately on my pressure gauge and the visibility. At such a low pressure, the gauge needle swung up and down with my breathing, so that after each breath I would watch to see how high the pressure reading came up to, which was less, and less, and less. As the needle began to swing lower and simply stay near the zero mark, I could just begin to be able to see a dark area where the ship's overhang was and a brighter area beside it — that was my way out! Now that I had something to aim for, I let go of the wreck and swam diagonally up for the surface as fast as I could (thinking "to hell" with the slow ascent we would normally make as a precaution against getting an air embolism, I was less than thirty feet down, I would take the risk).

I finally broke through the surface and gasped a big lung-full of fresh air. It had never tasted sweeter! Looking around, I spotted my dive buddy, who had been watching from our agreed meeting point, and waved. We had both made it back to the surface!

I tore off my mask, snorkel, and regulator and just floated on my back for a few minutes, drinking in that beautiful fresh air and looking up at the sky. Recriminations would come later. For now, I was happy we were both alive. Even so, I did have the grace to spare a thought of thanks for those two crusty sergeants, who had taught me more than I had realized.

* * *

The Bell Mine Headframe

Little did I know that those skills, developed years earlier, would come in handy once more in a completely different context. I hadn't been able to find Norm to take me out on the lake again, but Jim had a boat that he used to guide hunters and sports fishers. I had asked him to take me out to Bell Island, to see the site of the Bell Uranium Mine. Always willing to be helpful, Jim had immediately agreed and then followed-up with what seemed to be his favourite phrase: "It'll cost you though." I'd said, "Fine, make it your standard hourly guide's rate and write me a bill for it."

We had set out in his guide boat, an aluminum 21-foot Lund Tyee Offshore with a 165 hp outboard. Jim was cheap, but he didn't skimp on his equipment. We settled into the two heavily cushioned front seats behind the windshield, under a convertible roof, with his large outboard motor providing a steady roar. Thankfully, the lake was quite calm so it was an uneventful ninety-minute ride, leaving me to lean back and enjoy the beauty of one of Canada's largest and least travelled lakes. It struck me once again what a beautiful part of the country this was. To our right was nothing but water as far as the eye could see – we could just as well have been in the middle of an ocean. To our left, only a mile away was the shoreline with its rocky hills, beaches, and patches of forest, with an occasional trapper's cabin – reminders of the occasional presence of humans in this area. Looking ahead, it was the big wide-open blue sky that commanded my attention, with only a few clouds and the occasional bird or two to add scale to the expansive landscape.

Reaching the island, and making sure the boat was securely tied up, Jim led me into the forest along what looked like an old gravel roadway, now almost lost as mature trees leaned in and over it from each side, and bushes and small young trees resolutely pushed their way up through the gravel. Fifteen or twenty minutes of hiking brought us to a clearing on the far side of which was a fairly large hill with what looked like a cave entrance. As we got closer, it became clear that it wasn't a natural cave but rather a large entrance that had been blasted out from the side of the hill. At some point in the past, someone had installed a metal grate affair across the entrance to seal it off. It was rusty, with rough, reddish-brown surfaces indicating many years of corrosion, but it still looked strong to me.

"This is it?" I asked Jim, "This is the Bell Mine?"

"Not exactly," Jim replied, squinting at the grate as if to see what lay beyond. "This is what they call an adit – a passage that's been blasted into the side of a hill to provide access to the inner workings of the mine. Sometimes these adits were used as emergency exits too. The real mine entrance is higher up and on the other side of this hill. That's where the headframe used to be, where they would have hoisted the miners down into the mine, and lifted the mined ore up and out of the mine ... Now that we're here, what are we looking for?"

"I'm interested in any evidence of recent human activity. Any signs someone might have been opening up old entrances, collecting samples, or blasting – anything you wouldn't expect to find around a mine that's been abandoned for ten years," I replied. It was decided that I would investigate this adit, while Jim would go and have a look at another adit that he said was just around the side of the hill. Not without further negotiation, however. Following another "It'll cost you though," from Jim and a "Fine, whatever," from me, we agreed to meet at the main mine entrance on the far side of the hill in an hour.

We found that we could swing the grate out enough from one side for me to be able to squeeze by and get into the adit passageway. Jim said that it was safe for me to go in, but not to go in too far. As he started to hike around the hill to look at the next adit, he called back over his shoulder: "Go straight, don't go too far, don't take any side passages, and ..." The rest was lost to the breeze as I watched his blue plaid jacket waving in the wind as he disappeared around the side of the hill.

I went in. The walls just inside the entrance were extremely rough, as no attempt had been made to smooth the walls or ceiling. The early miners must have just blasted and pickaxed their way in, clearing away just enough rock to provide the access they needed. The floor was fairly smooth, although it was heavily cluttered with rocks and dust. I had had to step carefully around bits of rusty metal that appeared to have come from everything from pipes to machinery. The passageway had been shrinking as I went in deeper, and I had gone in just about as far as I felt comfortable going when I saw a lump of red. A red-ish cloth was either attached to or hanging on a wall a couple of feet off the ground, and it was just a few more yards ahead. I crept forward. Now there were occasional wooden planks on the floor, making it easier to walk. I was looking at the cloth, wondering what it was when there was a loud "crack - snap," and the floor gave way, right below my feet.

"Eeek!" I gave an involuntary squeal as I dropped. In an instant, I had fallen forward and into some kind of open shaft. Fortunately, the shaft was narrow, because some involuntary instinct had induced me to lean quickly forward, just barely in time to get my arms stretched out and over the rock floor on the other side so that I didn't fall in completely. On the other hand, it had left me with my arms out on the floor, my armpits pressed against the lip of the shaft, and all of the rest of me dangling into the abyss.

"DON'T PANIC!"

I had told myself that once before.

In my mind, I could once again hear the voices of my two SCUBA sergeants saying *Get a grip! Panic kills!* As I tried to implement this advice, my senses piled-on once more. I became alive to the cold surface of the rock face I was now hugging, the even colder air coming up the mine shaft below me, and the cool, inky darkness in whatever it was that lay before me.

OK, don't panic, I thought. *Take a few slow, calming breaths - and think!* I couldn't move much, but I didn't seem to be in immediate danger of falling in any further, so I took a minute to catch my breath. Time to inventory my surroundings and take stock of the situation.

The sharp edge of the shaft was cutting into my chest just below the armpits, but it was reassuring to feel something solid. I must have fallen into a raise. Jim had explained that vertical, or nearly vertical, openings in an underground mine were called "raises," and that they were usually constructed to provide access from one mining level to another or even all the way to the surface. The miners had clearly taken more care in the construction of this raise because the wall I was hugging was remarkably smooth. Raising one leg at a time as far as I dared, I tried to feel for a toe-hold of some kind but felt nothing. Try as I might, I couldn't feel anything that the toes or the sides of my boots could rest on.

With my arms extended and my armpits wedged tightly against the edge of the raise, I could keep myself from falling the rest of the way in, but I didn't have the strength to pull myself up and over the edge. I couldn't see or feel anything on the floor that I could grip with my hands or forearms and, with nothing to brace my boots on, I had no means of leverage there either.

"Help!" I tried yelling for help every few minutes, in hopes Jim might have wandered back this way, but I could only hear my own echoes. Calling out wasn't helping, and it was making me tire faster, so I eventually gave that up. I hadn't brought my service revolver with me, and I'm not sure I could have released one of my arms to try to get at it anyway.

Tired. I was feeling very tired ...

I was beginning to feel that my sergeants were letting me down, as I just couldn't visualize a pathway to saving myself this time.

At this point, I was about ready to try something riskier. If I could shuffle to the left or right maybe I could get to some kind of wall or protrusion that I could get a knee or boot on without loosening my grip on the rock or spending the last of my strength. Before I could try it, the silence of the mine was broken by an ear-splitting sound.

"*Grruph, Grruph, Grruph.*" Suddenly a huge hairy face, with piercing blue-grey eyes and jaws bearing large teeth, appeared. It felt like the eyes and teeth were rushing right at my face.

I involuntarily jumped, and so sharply that I felt like I was going to pop out of my skin, but part of my brain alerted me to keep my arms firmly on the rock so I wouldn't fall down the raise. Struggling to get a grip on this new terror, I realized that I was looking at a wolf. No, on second thought, it wasn't a wolf, it was a large dog – more like a Husky of some kind. Once I got my heart-rate back down (again!), and still staring literally eye-to-eye with this apparition, I got the strangest sense that he (it felt like a "he") wasn't so much threatening me as trying to get my attention.

Now that I could take a moment to examine him, I could see that he wasn't really baring his teeth at me, and he wasn't growling either. He barked a few more times, and then once he clearly had my attention he lowered his shoulders and put his head down on the rock, almost as if he was bowing or kneeling like a dog does to another dog to signal an invitation to play. I was pretty sure he didn't want to play. The tone of his bark seemed purposeful, serious. I looked into his eyes – I know that the advice books say not to stare directly into a strange dog's eyes but since I couldn't move, and he was right there, literally in my face, I didn't have a lot of other options. Anyway, as I looked into his eyes I suddenly got the distinct impression that he wanted me to grab his scruff, the fur at the back of his neck.

"You've got to be kidding me," I said out loud.

As we shared a gaze, all I could see in my mind was an image of me grabbing his fur so he could help me get up and over the edge of the raise. I dimly recalled reading somewhere or other that the right half of the brain was good at processing emotions and generating awareness of other people's mental states, but I'd never heard of it serving as a means of communication, certainly not between humans and animals, and I didn't believe in telepathy or the occult. Yet, I was getting weaker by the minute and colder now, too.

The dog was still very intent on me, alternating between barks to get my attention and bowing his head to show that he wasn't being aggressive. I really couldn't think of anything else to do, so I very slowly moved one forearm over to him and lifted my left hand up and on top of his neck. At this, he gave a sniff and kept staring at me, so I grabbed his fur with my left hand and moved my right arm slightly in preparation for a push upward. This produced a distinct snort as if to say "about time," and he braced himself and lifted his head and shoulders.

Unbelievably, he then started to shift his body back and I realized that this was actually a pretty big dog. With him shifting back and me levering up on my right arm I was able to rise up just a bit. At this point, he lowered his head again and this time closed those huge jaws on the collars of my shirt and jacket. Backing up once more with my collars in his jaws, and me holding on to him with my left hand and pushing up on the rock with my right arm, we moved a bit further. Pretty soon, I was able to essentially crawl with my elbows on the ground, while still holding onto his fur, and we continued to inch ever so slowly along the ground. Eventually, I got enough of my chest over the edge that I was able to catch a full breath, without too much fear of falling back over, and soon it was pretty easy to get my waist up and then bent over the edge. With a final swing, the last of me came over the top. Saved!

Once again, I found myself just lying on my back for a few minutes, drinking in that beautiful fresh air and looking up at … well, nothing really. The roof was just rough-hewn rock. But at that moment, it was as beautiful a sight as the broad blue sky had been. Maybe I should have been a geologist. *Thanks again, my two sergeants*, I thought. I turned to look at my saviour – who was sitting on his haunches looking at me – and said, "Thank you. I don't know where you came from, but thank you!"

Now, finally, I could go take a look at the lump of red-ish cloth that had drawn me so far into the adit in the first place. I found that it was a red felt jacket, hanging from a bit of protruding rock. As I rummaged through it, looking unsuccessfully for any contents or some means of identification, I detected an unusual odour. The musty lived-in smell of seldom-washed clothing, mixed with the scent I associated with the fur hats and gloves that I had seen the locals wearing. I knew that smell. It was like when I'd visited Norm in his trapper's cabin and he had shown me some of his stuffed-animal trophies.

Norm!

I was pretty sure that Norm had been here, but doing what? Now that I was able to reach the flashlight I had brought with me, I used it to look around, especially around the place where the ground had given way below me. I could see that there had been wooden beams, set beneath a thin cover of dirt and gravel. Looking closely at the projecting, broken ends of the beams I could see that they were partly smooth and partly fractured. Someone had deliberately set a trap!

Examining further, it looked like the boards covering the shaft had been removed, sawed most of the way through, and then replaced and covered over. If someone had seen the beams, they probably would have looked solid but weren't capable of holding up any significant weight. A deliberate attempt to injure or even kill someone.

Now I had more questions. Why would anyone set a trap here? Was it Norm? If so, it would have been foolish to leave his own jacket behind. If it was someone else that set the trap, then had Norm been shrewd enough, or lucky enough, to avoid the trap? Or had he been here before the trap had been set?

Cautiously advancing to the edge, I shone the beam down the raise I had nearly dropped into. It was a long way down, but the last traces of the beam's light were just able to show that the bottom only looked like more rock. Certainly nobody down there. Sweeping the light around, I failed to find anything else unusual, and I certainly had no intention of going down into the raise.

Meanwhile, where the hell had Jim been while I was living out my last few minutes of upper body strength hanging in that damn mine shaft? It was time to go find Jim. As the dog trotted along -

not close, but not far away - I found Jim where we had planned to meet, around the far side of the hill, sitting and smoking next to the ruins of what he called the mine's head-frame.

Jim was surprised to see that I was so tired out and amazed to hear my story. "Why didn't you call me?" he asked, which provoked an "I yelled like there was no tomorrow," from me. He explained that he'd found the next adit to be completely blocked, so he'd come all the way around the hill to the mine's main entrance and hadn't heard a thing. "You've had a lucky escape," he said, "the inner layouts of these old mines are long forgotten, and no two mines seem to be laid out in quite the same way." Jim was so apologetic about not hearing me that I waved it all off and asked about the dog.

"Him? Why that's Silver, one of Norm's sled dogs," he said. "Norm has a whole team of sled dogs, and Silver here is their leader. "I've heard of dogs rescuing small children before, but I never heard of a dog rescuing a Mountie," Jim chuckled. I showed him the jacket that I had found, which he allowed could be Norm's, and certainly looked like his.

"Why would Norm be out here poking around?" I wondered out loud. "Where is he? What is Norm's dog doing out here, all by himself on an island? Could Silver have swum out to the island?"

"He probably did," Jim said, "but I've never seen him in the water before." We searched around and called out several times, but there was no further sign of Norm.

It didn't take long for Jim and I to look at what was left of the mine and the island. The island wasn't very big, the second adit was blocked with rock, and the main shaft was covered with a secure-looking metal grate. With my flashlight, we could see that the shaft was flooded down below. Jim explained that flooding was natural in these old mines when there were no longer pumps running to take the water out.

As we searched around, I noticed that Silver would roam around, seemingly following his own interests, but he never strayed far from us. I would often see him turn to look at us as if making sure that he knew where we were, or perhaps where we were going. By the time we had seen everything, there was to see and had come full-circle back to the boat, I had resolved to try to bring Silver with us.

"Jim, do you think he'll come in the boat with us?" I asked. "I don't like the idea of leaving him marooned here on this island."

"He might come," Jim allowed, "but who's going to look after him until Norm shows up?"

"I will," I said firmly. He'd saved my life and I was not going to turn around and abandon him to the elements in the middle of nowhere.

"OK. It'll cost you though," Jim started to say, and then hastily added as he saw me start to flare up, "Cost you in dog food and whatnot, I mean."

"That's OK," I supplied, "he's earned all the dog food he can ever eat." We eased the bow of the boat into shallow water, I climbed in, turned, and called out "Come Silver, come jump in the boat!" To our surprise, he just padded down to the shore, gave Jim a glance, and jumped into the boat as if he'd been doing it all his life. Which, come to think of it, he probably had. I had expected Silver to be wary of us and wanting to stay behind to wait for his master. Maybe he'd had enough of waiting though because he showed no hesitation at coming with us.

As Jim directed the boat back towards Radium City, I offered Silver some of my lunch. In a flash, it was all gone. Although his demeanour and his coat seemed to be healthy, he was ravenously hungry and ate everything I offered. Eventually, he curled up on the seat behind me and immediately dropped-off to sleep. I had now acquired a marooned dog and a missing person. Being in a remote, almost uninhabited area, I wondered about the probability of encountering three mysteries in the same month. I had no reason to connect Norm or Silver to the two break-ins, beyond my suspicious nature, but I filed them away in my mind as being possibly connected, and I resolved to keep an open mind.

As we journeyed back, I once again gazed raptly out at the huge expanse of water, fully matched by the wide-open sky, and it occurred to me to wonder if the red jacket I'd found could symbolize something else: a red herring?

Silver

11 A NEW PARTNER

I drove out to Norm's place, but there was no trace of Norm. All of his sled dogs, except Silver, were gone. Like most northerners, Norm didn't keep his dogs tied up or fenced in, and the sled dogs could normally be seen prowling around town, playing in their yard, or lying on the tops of their individual dog houses – either napping or surveying their realms. Of course, the dogs could have been off prowling around town, and Norm could have been off hunting, or doing any of a million other things, but my suspicions were aroused now. Otherwise, Norm's house seemed undisturbed.

Driving around town, I saw what looked like some of Norm's dogs hovering around the back of Ruby's café (mooching for food?). When I stopped by the marina, I found that Norm's boat was still moored in its usual berth.

Unsure about what to do with Silver, I decided to keep him with me for the time being. Mike had agreed with me and said he was fine with Silver staying at the detachment as long as I took responsibility for him. This was an easy thing to accomplish as Silver seemed to be sticking with me like glue.

Silver padded around the detachment, sniffing in every nook and cranny, but he seemed satisfied with his new surroundings. That evening, he accompanied me on my foot patrol around town, and I found that I enjoyed his company. Honesty compels me to admit that I also felt safer having him with me, as I had not fully shaken-off the effects of being jumped in the bookstore only two days before, and then nearly dying in a mine shaft the previous day.

Later that night, although he must have been an "outdoor dog," he put up an awful fuss when I tried to leave him in the yard. Still very much feeling indebted to him, I let him stay inside with me, and he quickly claimed the foot of my bed as his own.

The next day, Silver had immediately joined me in a morning run, a habit that was a legacy of all the running I'd had to do in my police training. With no real gym in town, I had developed the habit of jogging around town early in the morning, roughly every second day of the week. By picking more or less random running routes, I had gotten to know the look and feel of the whole town this way, and the townspeople had gotten to know me by sight if nothing else. Another small step forward in building community-police relations. Silver quickly followed suit. I soon found that he would try to join me in everything I did. In this case, he would lope off in his own directions from time to time, to investigate interesting smells - presumably to get a sense of what the other dogs in town had been up to. Finding one, he'd lift a leg to deposit a small scent message to let others know he'd been there too, and then finally run back, catch-up to me, and trot along companionably until the next interesting spot came along. As much as I was used to being alone, I found that I really enjoyed his quiet company.

I had hoped for an early-morning trip to look around the Fish Hook Bay area mine sites, but these could only be accessed by air or water. Unfortunately, it was too rough to go out on the big lake that day, so I had to postpone the trip. As it was too early to be knocking on doors around town, I cleaned-up the Detachment ("fatigues" again!), finished up the day's administrative duties. After that, accompanied by Silver, I tried talking to people around town. By mid-afternoon, my asking around to see whether anyone had seen Norm lately had been spectacularly unsuccessful.

I had just about convinced myself that I was worrying needlessly about Norm and that I should simply wait to see whether he or any news of him turned up when Ruby came running up to me.

"I'm worried about Norm," she exclaimed, "He does odd jobs for me around the café. He was supposed to have done things for me over the past two days but hasn't shown up. I went out to his place several times, but he hasn't been there either. No one around town has seen him, and I'm getting worried."

"What's Silver hanging around here for?" she asked, noticing that he had been sitting nearby, watching us.

I told her that I'd been looking for Norm too, that he hadn't taken his boat out either, and that Silver had been following me around for some reason.

"When did you last see Norm?" I asked.

"Last time I saw him was two days ago, Tuesday morning, at about 11 am, when he came in for lunch at the café."

I took down all the details Ruby could give me, and told her I would file a missing person report. As the two of us walked back to her café, I asked her to let me know right away if she heard anything from anyone else about Norm, and I promised to keep looking and asking around myself. When we got there, Ruby's café was deserted except for Ron McGee, who was sitting in a booth, nursing a cup of coffee. As I went over to join him, I noticed that there was a saucer of milk or cream sitting in front of him, even though he took his coffee black. This mystery, at least, was soon solved as the question forming on my lips was pre-empted by the emergence from his jacket of the small white and black head of his cat, Ally, who stretched herself out to take a few licks of cream before disappearing back into Ron's jacket. Ron may not have been much of a "people person" but he sure was attached to his cat.

"The cat's not really allowed in here," Ron explained, "but no one has ever minded as long as I keep her tucked away."

"She's obsessed with food," Ron continued, "I think she must have been a stray at one time because once they've gone starving they tend to eat every chance that they get ... she even wakes me up with her meowing in the middle of the night because she's afraid of going hungry," Ron explained.

I was too worried about Norm to bother with the cat and simply asked Ron if he'd seen Norm around anywhere. Like Ruby, he too had seen Norm two days earlier, in the café, but not since.

I didn't want to over-react, but as I asked around town, it soon became clear that no one else had seen or heard from Norm since Tuesday morning either. Returning to the detachment, I filed a Missing Person report by telex.

```
M
0535 EST+
RCMP PR ALBERT
V
VIA WUI+
RCMP PR ALBERT

RCMP RADCITY

PRIORITY

FM: RADIUM CITY DET.
TO: PR ALBERT S/DIV
BT
UNCLAS

MISSING PERSON REPORTED BY RUBY GILLESPIE, AGE 45, APPEARS TO
BE SINCERE. REPORTED MISSING IS NORMAN VINCENT POOLE, AGE 40,
AKA NORM, RESIDENT OF RADIUM CITY. LAST SEEN R. CITY, ON 9
SEPT, AT 11 AM. INVESTIGATING.
ELS.
+
RCMP PR ALBERT

RCMP RADCITY
VVV
```

***

Talking things over with Mike in the hospital that evening, he remarked that I seemed to have a new partner. I hadn't even noticed that Silver had followed me into the hospital, and the staff had let him get away with it too.

"He won't leave me," I said, "but I have to admit that I do like having him around."

"Well, I feel better knowing that you're not alone on your patrols right now, especially with all your mysteries piling up. A bit of volunteer back-up could be better than none until Dr. Evans lets me out of here."

That night Silver and I did a walking patrol together, and more than one person compared us to Hollywood's Sergeant Preston and his dog, Yukon King. It wasn't that Silver really stuck to me like glue. He would run off and sniff around, keep an eye on any other dogs in range of his senses, and sometimes simply run ahead. On the other hand, he never wandered far away, and never seemed to lose track of where I was, or what I was doing. Catching him gazing up at me with his penetrating blue-grey eyes, I began to wonder whether he was actively protecting me for some reason.

I wasn't sure whether to be relieved or disappointed that there were no more suspicious incidents that night.

The next morning, I went to see Andrew again, in his office at the bank. Silver had slipped in with me, and as I apologized and made to shoo him outside, Andrew waved me off.

"We don't normally allow dogs in the bank, but silver is always welcome here ... get it? 'Silver?' ..." I'd found another comedian.

Getting down to business, I related some of my investigations and adventures, and my discussion with Norm about mines and stocks. At this, Andrew gave a slow whistle. "So, you think there's gold to be had in the old Bell Mine, and someone's killed off poor Norm to get at it?"

That was exactly what I thought, but I hadn't planned on letting Andrew that far into my confidence, and I was more than a little disconcerted at how quickly he had leaped to the same hypothesis. I hadn't even shared my suspicion that the mine shaft Silver had rescued me from had been a trap set for poor Norm.

In for a penny ..., I thought. "What about Norm's father's share certificates?" I asked. "Could someone steal them and cash them in?"

"No. They would have been registered in Norm's father's name or, if Norm inherited them he probably had the registrations transferred to his name. If someone stole them they'd be out of luck."

"A dead end then," I mused.

"Yes, unless he had option certificates or stock purchase warrants. Those would allow anyone to buy shares at the prices listed on the certificates, but even if they exist they would have had expiry dates, and it's unlikely that any would still be valid.'"

"Would you be able to check?"

"Sure, I'll call my broker in Winnipeg. Which Bell mine are you interested in?"

"WHAT?" I exclaimed, straightening up in my chair. "What do you mean 'which' Bell mine?"

"There were two. People usually just refer to the one on Bell Island, because the island and the old headframe serves as an unofficial navigation marker in the area. But there was a second Bell Mine fairly close by. It was on the mainland, just north of Fish

Hook Bay. When both mines were bought out, they became part of Consolidated Bell Mines and the company referred to them as the Bell-A and Bell-B mines, but most people just refer to 'Bell Mine,' meaning the one on the island with the headframe."

"Can you check on both?" I asked.

"Sure," he replied, picking up his phone and dialling.

While Andrew called his broker, I was mentally replaying my conversations with Norm and Jim. Neither had mentioned a second mine. Now, Norm was missing. I made a mental note to go check on Jim, just to be on the safe side.

When Andrew got off the phone he looked puzzled. "Well, someone must really have had optimism or faith, because there are still stock purchase warrants outstanding, under the name Consolidated Bell Mines, which still exists and still owns both the Bell-A and Bell-B mines."

"Wow, the plot thickens!"

"Yes, but there's one more thing ... the last of the warrants expire on the 30th of this month. I don't know why they allowed them to remain in force for so many years, but whatever the reason, their time is almost up."

"So now we have a reason for someone to be in a rush," I mused. "That could explain a lot, ... and that rush is probably still on if they're after those warrants. What's involved in exercising them?"

"You'd have to have the physical certificates in hand and deliver them to a registered stock broker's office before the expiry date. I'd suggest two business days before, to allow time for the broker to make all the arrangements."

"OK, so today is the 12th and they'd need to be delivered to somewhere like Saskatoon or Winnipeg by, say, Friday the 26th if the broker needs until the following Monday to make the necessary arrangements. If we're right about all this, that gives our hypothetical mystery person exactly two weeks. This is going to get more interesting before we're done!"

Thanking Andrew, and swearing him to absolute secrecy about all this once again, I took my leave. I wasn't more than five feet outside the bank before Silver silently appeared by my side and brushed up against my leg by way of announcing his presence.

"Well Silver," I said, "it's time to go visit one more abandoned uranium mine."

"Grruph," he said.

"Yes, we'll need to be very careful this time."

Mike didn't want me to go, but I convinced him that we might be running out of time. He couldn't be released from the hospital yet, and we didn't have sufficient basis to ask Prince Albert Sub-Division to send official backup. We also agreed that, while I didn't seriously suspect Jim, we should avoid raising his curiosity any further, and that I'd get someone else to take me out.

"Ask Horace," Mike said.

"The Mayor?"

"Yes, he's not a professional guide, but he's a keen boater, hunter, and fisherman, and he grew up around here, so he knows the geography. He can read the water, and he can read the weather. He'll be a good choice, … unless he's our mystery person – so be careful, and promise me you won't go without Silver."

"Silver?"

"Yes, he's a smart dog, he's a leader, and he's obviously attached himself to you." Then, looking over at Silver, who was half-sleeping, curled up in a corner, "I wouldn't like to be in his bad books if I could help it. Right Silver?"

"Grruph," he said, more loudly this time.

"I can't believe we're having these conversations with him … come on deputy Silver. Tomorrow, we hunt!" I only got a few feet towards the hospital ward's door when a sharp word from Mike brought me up short.

"Alex!!" he called, and then as I turned with eyebrows raised,

"Go armed!"

12 THE GUIDE IS FOUND

In my SCUBA diving days, I had once been visiting friends in Halifax and we had all gone out for a boat dive just outside the extreme mouth of the Halifax harbour. If that sounds like a place where the water would have been calm, it wasn't. On this particular day, the water was especially rough. As soon as we had left the relatively protected waters of the inner harbour and passed McNabs Island the swell increased and our dive boat began to bob up and down more and more violently with each wave.

As we continued outward, the boat began to roll as well. It was the twisting motion of the pitching and rolling, that soon had two of my friends turning green and heading for the gunwales in search of a place to throw up.

Our skipper insisted that it was still safe to go on, but he allowed that we could turn back if we wanted to. Being students at the time, we were relatively rich in terms of spare time but not in terms of money, and we were going to have to pay for the boat trip either way – so that provided a reason to keep going. Besides, we were after big game. The goal of this trip was to find the wreck of a World War II fighter plane that was believed to have crashed into the ocean just outside the harbour entrance.

With this in mind, the consensus was to continue. By the time we reached the dive site and dropped anchor, a third friend was down with sea-sickness and I was concentrating on keeping my eyes firmly focused on the horizon while trying to keep my stomach in place. By the time the anchor was set, there were only four of us able to dive. We would go in as pairs, one pair at a time. When my dive buddy and I entered the water and dropped below the waves, we silently rejoiced. The water below the waves almost immediately became relatively calm, and all feelings of pending sickness quickly vanished.

Following the anchor rope to the bottom, we scoured the area around it as best we could in the limited visibility. This was done by swimming in a search pattern of concentric circles, using a separate rope linked to the anchor rope as a guide. When our air ran low we came up to change air tanks (courtesy of our companions who were unable to dive and couldn't use theirs) and searched again without success. When two tanks each had been used up, we had essentially also used up our available "no-decompression" bottom time, so we had to give up the search for the fighter plane.

The trip back to Halifax was slightly less stressful, and the four of us that "survived" were able to joke about being able to use the tanks of our less fortunate companions, but my main takeaway memory was of how close I had come to being violently seasick myself.

***

Now I was experiencing the same thing all over again, this time on Lake Athabasca.

I'd certainly had no trouble convincing Horace to take me out to the Bell-B mine. He was impressed that I knew the difference between the two Bell mines and told me that they had been an important part of Radium City's history, one of them having had the distinction of being the first uranium discovery in all of Saskatchewan. He seemed more than happy to have Silver along too, as I explained that I'd still had no success locating Norm and that in the meantime I was looking after Silver.

This was my third venture out on Lake Athabasca, and it was nothing like the previous two trips. The wind was blowing hard, and even though we stayed close inshore and Horace had us duck around islands every chance he could, the waves were high and angry. I hadn't realized that waves could get so violent on an inland lake. Horace explained that on such large lakes when the wind blew out of the wrong direction, which wasn't very often, it had lots of time and space to build dangerous waves. That's what it was doing now, and with a vengeance.

Silver had curled up in the lowest part of the boat, and very near its centre. *That's a very smart dog,* I thought, not for the first time. Meanwhile, the boat continued to hammer against each wavefront in turn, and I was remembering my Halifax experience. Once again, I tried to use the tricks of concentrating my eyes on the horizon and mentally trying to keep my stomach in place, but memories of having barely pulled this off before were not helping me. As if my stomach wasn't enough, I was starting to worry about my back, which was feeling each and every blow radiate up from my bottom to my neck.

I could see that Horace was doing his best to moderate the effects of the waves. He constantly adjusted the throttle to try to match the speed of the boat to the frequency of the wave crests, but every time he succeeded we'd get only a brief reprieve, lasting a couple of wavefronts at most, before the frequency of the waves changed and he'd have to adjust yet again. This happened over, and over on the two and a half hours, it took us to reach Bell Island and then land and tie-up on the shore of Fish Hook Bay. It was such a relief to beach the boat and escape the waves that we just sat and rested for a while, admiring the beautiful scenery and allowing our internal systems to get back to some kind of balance again.

From the shore, it was a bit of a hike inland. We followed an old road that was barely visible, it was so heavily overgrown with bushes and trees. This made our progress slow and sweaty, despite the fact that we were now into the coolness of early fall, northern weather.

As we trudged along, pausing now and again to consult our map and compass, I was just about ready to call for a rest stop when a loud bark broke the relative stillness of the forest. Silver had gone from padding along slightly ahead of us, to giving out a ringing bark and then taking off at full speed ahead, along the road we'd been following.

"What's got into him?" Horace asked as we heard a furious barking coming from somewhere up ahead of us.

"No idea," I responded. "Maybe he's cornered a skunk, or a bear or something."

As we finally emerged from the forest, we found ourselves looking at the entrance to an old mine adit. Silver was standing in front of a rusty old iron grate that was covering the entrance, and still barking furiously.

"OK Silver. Stay! Calm down, and we'll go take a look together." Silver seemed to understand me because he obediently sat on his haunches and watched us.

As we examined the iron grate, we found that the whole thing was secured by four bolts that had been driven into the rock.

The Bell-B Mine

The rock face itself looked like granite, so we weren't likely to be able to dig the bolts out, and we didn't have the tools to try unscrewing them. There was quite a bit of mine debris laying around, however, and we were able to find an eight-foot length of solid-looking angle-iron we could use as a lever, and a boxy-shaped piece of iron we could use as a fulcrum.

With me holding the makeshift fulcrum, Horace positioned the angle-iron to pry the grate away from its bolts on one side and put all of his strength and energy into a huge push of our makeshift lever toward the rock face. This turned out to have been completely unnecessary, as with a sharp cry he flew into the rock face itself. At the same time, the other end of the lever came away from the grate and would have caught me in the neck or head if not for the fact that the sudden and unexpected motion had caused me to promptly fall to the ground. We both laughed sheepishly as we picked ourselves up, and then we both looked at the mine entrance in wonder. The side of the grate had come completely free!

"Someone's been through here before us," Horace exclaimed. "Look at the bolts."

Both of the large lag bolts on one side had popped out of the rock when the grate came free, and we found that when we tried replacing them in the rock they just slid right in without having to be turned.

"Someone was through here, and then put the grate back and pushed the bolts into the holes so everything would look normal, even though it wasn't," Horace concluded, as he showed me how he could wiggle each bolt in the holes in the rock.

The other side of the grate seemed secure in the rock, so Horace and I put our weight behind the free edge and pushed the grate more and more open until we were rewarded with a loud scraping sound and a metallic popping sound. This time, the remaining two bolts had stayed in the rock, but the grate had come right off. We laid the grate aside, and I quickly called Silver to stop as he had poised himself to run inside.

Once again, Silver paused, and sat on his hind legs, looking at me expectantly.

"We'll go in together – slowly ... OK?"

"Does he really understand what you're saying?" Horace asked.

"I have no idea. Maybe he's very well trained, but sometimes it seems like he can read my mind."

Both Horace and I had brought flashlights with us, so we switched them on and entered carefully, with me holding onto Silver's ruff to remind him not to leap ahead. I wasn't sure that Silver would let me get away with holding on to him, but he seemed content. After my previous Bell Mine experience, it was impossible for me to avoid thinking about falling into an open shaft, giving me a second reason to hang on to Silver, and I wondered if he could sense that.

In we went.

The three of us proceeded cautiously along the narrow, low passageway, being careful not to overstep the illumination from our flashlights. It was dark and damp, and I could feel a current of cold air coming from somewhere ahead - presumably a lower level of the workings. The cold air felt nice after our lengthy hike, but I wondered what the radiation level was, and that we probably shouldn't explore inside for very long without getting it tested first.

We soon came to a three-way junction and paused to consider whether to proceed straight ahead or take one of the side tunnels.

"Which way do you want to go?" Horace asked.

Silver had been sniffing very diligently as we had made our way into the mine, and he now began to make whimpering sounds as he pulled me toward the right-hand tunnel.

"Silver smells something," I replied, "and he wants us to go this way – let's give it a try."

We had only gone about three feet into the side tunnel, when our flashlights illuminated two lines on the floor, spaced about a foot apart, leading ahead. In about fifteen more feet, the lines ended at a pair of boots. The boots had feet in them. We had found poor Norm!

Silver immediately went up to Norm's face and gave him a good sniff and then a couple of licks, before sitting down with a low whine.

"I'm sorry Silver," I said, as even in the poor light of our flashlights I could see that Norm's skin had turned an unhopeful grey colour. I felt for his body temperature – cold, like the rock. I checked for a pulse – nothing. "I'm afraid Norm is gone."

We found that *rigor mortis* was still partially set-in when we turned his body over, revealing the cause of death - the lower back of his skull had been crushed.

"Looks like he'd been hit with something fairly large," I murmured, mostly to myself. "Could have been a rock or a large tree branch ..."

"How about the *rigor mortis?*," Horace asked.

There were two answers to this.

"We'll have to ask Dr. Evans," I said out loud. This was the truth, but not the whole truth.

In my own mind, I remembered being taught that *rigor mortis* is usually fully set-in by about 13 hours after death and that it starts relaxing after another 50 to 60 hours. That added up to something like 73 hours. In the cold confines of the mine, I suspected that it would take longer than that. Norm was last seen in town on Tuesday, about 84 hours previously. So, according to my mental math, whenever Norm was killed, it wasn't a lot later than that. He almost certainly died later on the same day that he was last seen. All of this I kept to myself.

"It looks like he's been dragged in here, so I bet he was killed somewhere else," Horace's voice brought my thoughts back to the present.

"Yes, I think so too," I said. "I wonder if he came here from Bell Island," I mused.

"Why Bell Island?"

I told Horace about my adventure on Bell Island, and how I'd found Silver, and a jacket I believed to be Norm's, on the island only a few days earlier.

Horace whistled softly, "So he might have met up with someone here or on Bell Island."

"Yes, but I'm inclined to suspect Bell Island because otherwise, I can't figure out why Silver was left there." I don't think we'll learn too much more today, but at least we have some new things to go on."

Sure enough, although we searched the other two mine passageways, and then searched back the way we had come, there seemed to be no more clues to find. Certainly, there was no sign of a struggle anywhere, and nothing in the nature of a bloody murder weapon. It took the rest of the afternoon for us to carry Norm out of the mine, and back to the boat, where we covered him with an old blanket of Horace's. It was evening by the time we were able to deliver Norm to the hospital for Dr. Evans to take a look at him.

I still didn't see Horace as a realistic suspect, and the shock on his face when we'd found Norm had seemed genuine. I did, however, take the precaution of swearing him to secrecy for the time being, as I'd done before with Andrew.

Silver came along with me, as always. I think he understood that poor Norm was gone forever.

The next day, I went to see Dr. Evans, and we held an impromptu meeting in the ward, sitting around Mike's bed. He confirmed the cause of death as being massive trauma due to a blunt force injury to the lower back of the head, and he gave me a copy of his death certificate. Given the circumstances, we decided that I should go and search Norm's place for clues, before going to see the town's two lawyers.

Norm's place had not been broken-into the last time I'd been there, but it had certainly been broken-into more recently. While Silver went off to visit with some of Norm's dogs in the yard, I went in. Surveying the various rooms, things seemed more or less intact but in disarray. It seemed like the place had been pretty thoroughly searched, including furniture pulled-out and pictures askew, suggesting a search for a safe or strong-box of some kind. It was a locking four-drawer filing cabinet in a basement office that seemed to have received the most attention. The locked drawers had been forced open, probably with the large crowbar that was lying nearby on the floor. All four drawers had been pulled out and searched, and there was a large folder of stock certificates lying on the floor. Most of the stock certificates were for shares in Consolidated Bell Mines and had Norm's name printed on them. There was also a large, accordion-style file folder lying empty on the floor nearby. I wondered what had been in the empty file folder, especially since it represented the only evidence of anything having actually been stolen.

Not finding anything else, I photographed each part of the house that showed signs of the intruder and then tried dusting the most obvious locations for fingerprints. Places like the door, filing cabinet, and file folders had been wiped clean of fingerprints. I gathered up the file of stock certificates, two more files that seemed to contain legal and broker correspondence regarding Norm's investments, and the crowbar. Making my way out, I secured the entrance to Norm's house and locked the evidence away in the trunk of our detachment's blue and white patrol car. I watched to see if Silver would want to stay behind with his pack mates, but he raced over as soon as he saw me open the car's door, and jumped right in to come with me.

My afternoon plan was to visit Radium City's two lawyers, in hopes of finding a will. The first lawyer was Mervyn J. Crowe, who was very much like the stereotype of a small-town lawyer. He was elderly, slow-moving, slow-speaking, and very reserved - to the point of being disengaged and aloof. His office, which was located at one extreme end of the town's main street, was a perfect match for him. The walls were almost completely covered with wooden bookcases filled with dusty looking books having dull-coloured spines, lettered in small print. The only parts of the walls not covered with bookcases were a small multi-paned window and an antique railway-station clock that was clearly still in working condition, with its pendulum swinging and a regular "tick, tick" on the extreme ends of each swing. The floor was fully covered with a faded carpet, on which were placed two antique hardwood chairs and a large oak desk. You could almost imagine a hush unfolding as you entered, with the carpet silencing even your footsteps. I explained why I was there and, despite receiving a solemn lecture on solicitor-client privilege, I was eventually able to drag out of him that no, Norm had not ever been a client of his. Wow, a classic character for sure. Leaving his office, I re-acquired Silver (who certainly had no chance of being admitted to that office) and we strolled down the main street to visit lawyer #2, whose office was located (really, I'm not making this up) at the extreme other end of the main street.

It was a sign. Not only were the two lawyers' offices located at the opposite ends of the town, they were just about opposite in personality too. Franklin P. Heath, "Please, call me Frank," turned out to be a middle-aged, former big-city corporate lawyer, and an extrovert. Frank explained that he had moved to Radium City several years earlier in an attempt to get away from the "rat race."

"The best decision I ever made was to get away from the rat-eating-rat worlds of Toronto and New York and hide out up here," Frank asserted with a chuckle.

In complete contrast to Mervyn J. Crowe's almost claustrophobia-inducing office, Frank's was very modern, bright, and open. He had several large windows, lots of lighting, and a tiled floor with petal-shaped chairs, and laminated wood office furniture. His decorations were brightly coloured and he had a nice-looking modern stereo with bookshelf speakers and cassette-deck playing background music. Shortly into our meeting, I realized that he'd been playing Elton John's *Greatest Hits* album, which had just recently been released. He seemed to be quite the modern person, with a sense of humour to match.

I'd asked him if there was enough work in town to support two lawyers, and whereas Mervyn J. Crowe would have been offended by such a question, Frank was amused.

"We lawyers have a saying," Frank answered, "One lawyer in town goes broke. Two lawyers in town get rich!"

I tried but failed to imagine Mervyn J. Crowe espousing such a saying.

When I explained the purpose of my visit, Frank immediately switched to a very helpful and competent-seeming lawyer mode. He'd already heard about Norm going missing and then being found dead. Frank confirmed that yes, Norm had been a client and that yes there was a will. He'd helped Norm revise his will about a year or two ago.

I gave Frank a copy of the death certificate and asked if I could see the will. Frank said that he couldn't give me the will just yet, citing client confidentiality, but that he could tell me what I wanted to know.

"Basically, Norm bequeathed everything to Ruby Gillespie: the house, his truck and boats, his dogs, and everything else, except for instructing that his estate cover his funeral and some minor debts."

"Why Ruby?"

"Well, he had no next of kin, and Norm and Ruby were really quite close, you know. They were more than employer-employee, more than just casual friends. How much more, I don't know. I didn't ever ask. I was curious, naturally, but I didn't need to know so I didn't come right out and ask him. 'Live and let live,' I always say."

I asked whether Ruby knew about all this, and he said that he assumed so, but didn't know for sure. In any case, he was going to go and see her right away to tell her, so she could start thinking about the decisions she was going to have to make and to see whether she would need any help from him.

I told Frank about the break-in at Norm's house and asked whether he had mentioned specific securities in his will. Frank said he hadn't, that he'd simply referred to having bank accounts and investments, but that a list might show up in Norm's effects somewhere. I gave him the folders of stock certificates and correspondence that I salvaged, for safekeeping, and I promised to get him the break-in report when I had it completed.

Knowing that Frank was heading over to see Ruby right away, I decided that I'd wait until the next day before going to see her.

The next day, it was quiet in Ruby's café after the breakfast rush subsided and we had a chance to sit at a corner table and have a quiet talk.

"Norm and I were very close. We grew up together," she explained, "beginning with going to the old school at the Gunnar mine's town-site, near where our parents worked. Our fathers both worked at the Gunnar mine back then, and our mothers worked at the Gunnar hospital. Our fathers weren't friends, particularly, but our mothers were, and eventually, we were too ... just friends, but good friends. After we'd grown up, we stayed friends and looked out for each other. We did some trips together, and Norm was always there to help me with things that needed doing around the café. I paid him for that, but money wasn't the reason he helped me out," she finished, wiping away a tear.

Frank's announcement the day before, that she was going to inherit Norm's estate, had come as a surprise, but not a huge surprise once she'd thought about it since she had known that Norm no longer had any living relatives. She said that Frank had explained everything to her, but "It's all a blur in my mind right now, so I'm going to have to go back in a while and get Frank to explain it all to me again."

Spotting Silver lurking about in front of the café's main bay window, Ruby said she was not a dog person, really, although she did feed them scraps from the back of her kitchen from time to time. She'd also been going out to Norm's place and feeding them every day that Norm had been missing. She didn't want to keep them permanently though, and she thought that she'd probably sell the sled dogs to a musher she knew quite well that lived in Skagway, Alaska.

"Silver too?" I tried to ask casually.

"No," she said. Then, with a kindly smile on her face, and having correctly interpreted my unsuccessful attempt to sound professionally neutral, she said "Norm and Silver got along all right but they were never really very close. Silver was a great lead dog, and that's all Norm wanted from him."

"Silver must be nearly three years old now and in all that time, they never became as close as you two have in less than a week," she said, looking through the window at where Silver had curled up outside on the sidewalk. Something tells me you two need to be together, so I'll tell you what I'll do ..."

"Yes?" I asked, in a low voice.

"I'll sign Silver over to you as soon as Frank gets all the legal niceties sorted out. Just promise me one thing."

"What's that?"

"You find Norm's killer and bring him to justice. Do it for Norm, and ... for all of us. Shake on it?"

"Ruby, I have to tell you that I'm already resolved to solve this thing anyway, but I'm not going to argue with you!" We shook hands with a solemnity that would have befitted a major business corporation's transaction. "And thank you for Silver, he's become my first real partner."

I was feeling quite whimsical as I took my leave of the café, and for some reason, it reminded me of the ending of the 1942 movie *Casablanca*. So, having stepped out onto the sidewalk I stopped, took a serious stance looking down at Silver, with my feet spread apart, and my hands on my hips, and I said,

"Silver, I think this is the beginning of a beautiful friendship!"

Laurie Schramm

13 THE TRAIL GETS WARM

Having met with Ruby right after lunch, I went over to the hospital to meet with Mike in hopes of reviewing the whole case with him. As a preliminary step, I had written out two lists in an attempt to organize my thoughts. So far, I had:

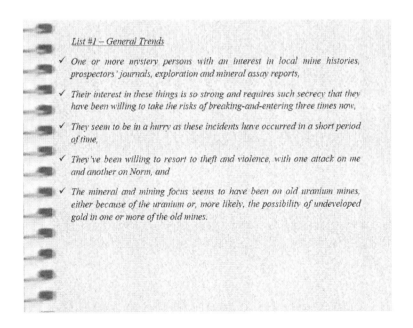

List #1 – General Trends

✓ One or more mystery persons with an interest in local mine histories, prospectors' journals, exploration and mineral assay reports,

✓ Their interest in these things is so strong and requires such secrecy that they have been willing to take the risks of breaking-and-entering three times now,

✓ They seem to be in a hurry as these incidents have occurred in a short period of time,

✓ They've been willing to resort to theft and violence, with one attack on me and another on Norm, and

✓ The mineral and mining focus seems to have been on old uranium mines, either because of the uranium or, more likely, the possibility of undeveloped gold in one or more of the old mines.

> *List #2 – The "Norm" Connection*
>
> ✓ *Although possibly not the whole story the Norm connection is, at least, quite specific, with actionable leads;*
>
> ✓ *Norm's father had been a part owner of a uranium mine that, together with a couple of other mines, ultimately became Consolidated Bell Mines Ltd.;*
>
> ✓ *Of those mines, I found Norm's jacket and Silver at the old Bell-A mine, and Norm's body at the old Bell-B mine, suggesting that he had been looking around one or both of these before falling victim to foul play;*
>
> ✓ *Norm's father had left him his shares in the company, which was still listed on the stock exchange, although it was trading at a very low share price;*
>
> ✓ *The share certificates at Norm's house had not been stolen, presumably because they were registered with a broker and the stock exchange, making the paper certificates themselves practically worthless;*
>
> ✓ *Norm's father may have also left him stock purchase warrants for Consolidated Bell Mines, but the warrants expire very soon (on Sept. 30th);*
>
> ✓ *It might be these warrants that were stolen from Norm's home, if so, the thief only had until the end of the month to use them to buy shares in the company – that would explain the need for speed;*
>
> ✓ *The share price for exercising the warrants is fixed by the terms on the certificates, but if the same person or persons were also buying shares on the market, then they wouldn't want any news about gold potential to get out until they'd bought their shares, so the stock price wouldn't shoot up until they had their stake secured – that would explain the need for secrecy.*

As Mike and I discussed the case, we both thought it probable that our murderer, or murderers, had set the trap in the Bell Island mine specifically for Norm. That trap had been intended to kill, but it hadn't worked. Norm must have avoided it, whether intentionally or accidentally while checking out the adit and left his jacket behind. Instead, the trap had caught me, but I'd survived.

"Why would Norm have gone to the mine in the first place?" I wondered.

"Someone may have started asking questions about the Bell mines, either asking Norm directly or asking others causing rumours to circulate," offered Mike. "That might have been enough to cause him to go and look for any signs of recent activity, like surveying or sampling."

"If so, then our murderer may have seen Norm on the island, gone over to see what he was up to at the Bell-A mine, and taken him over to the Bell-B mine – either dead or alive," I speculated, "and if our murderer was well enough known to Norm he might not have been suspicious of him, and might have willingly gone with the murderer over to the Bell-B mine, possibly leaving Silver behind with the intention of coming back for him later."

"In that case, whoever did it must have killed Norm then gone back for his boat, purposely left Silver marooned, and towed the boat from Bell Island back to its usual mooring in the Radium City marina. It would probably have been done late at night when it would have been unlikely for anyone to notice," mused Mike. "I think you should check his boat again, this time to see if the boat's wheel and controls have been wiped clean of fingerprints."

"Right. Even if the prints have been wiped clean that alone will tell us that we're on the right track."

"You're doing well Alex," Mike concluded, "I think you have a good handle on the What, Where, When, and the Why, so now we need the Who and we'll need some proof!"

Mike's preferred suspect was Ron McGee, and that was certainly a possibility as Ron was very knowledgeable about the mines and the metals they contained, and their values. This made him a natural suspect. I had no reason to eliminate him as a suspect, but something about it didn't feel right. Ron was probably shrewd enough to figure out the gold angle, but I didn't think that he had. In every encounter I'd had with him, he displayed a single-minded focus on uranium. It also occurred to me, rather uncharitably, that Mike might have been a bit biased against Ron - as Mike didn't like cats! But if not Ron, then who?

"Well, ..." I started to say, thinking it through, "It's probably someone with a boat or at least frequent access to a boat ..."

Mike gave me a meaningful look.

"OK, so that narrows it down to most of Radium City," I admitted, "and it could take forever to check everyone out ..."

"Unless ..." we both said at the same time.

"Unless we set a trap," I finished the thought, "Can we do that?"

"Entrapment – no," said Mike, and then steepled his hands and fingers together, preparatory to delivering a judgement, "but in this case, the trap wouldn't be aimed at tricking someone into committing a crime, it would be aimed at exposing our murderer. I think that kind of trap is quite justified in this case."

"A trap ..." I murmured, thoughtfully ...

Laurie Schramm

14 A TRAP IS SET

> When a Constable has concluded that an arrest should be made, they must proceed with the utmost determination to accomplish that purpose. Nothing short of imminent danger to the Constable's life will excuse failing to effect the arrest and hold the prisoner.
>
> ARRESTS. "RCMP CONSTABLES' MANUAL." OTTAWA

The next morning, I was "chomping at the bit," as they say, to do more investigating, but my top priority now had to be planning, rather than physical activity.

While continuing to ponder our next steps, I still had to look after routine detachment business, and I decided that I should get a licence for Silver as well. This created some high amusement at my expense for our mayor, Horace.

Having gone to the town office, I once again found that Mayor Horace Best was the only one on duty.

"You want what?" he asked, incredulously.

"A dog licence. For Silver."

"You want a dog licence for Silver," he repeated, in wonder, and then he started chuckling, "Have you seen how many dogs there are prowling around this town?" he asked.

"Sure."

"Do you have any idea how many of them are licensed?"

"No, I guess not," I admitted.

"Try none," he said, shifting from chuckling to outright laughter.

"Didn't you have a dog by-law back when Radium City had 5,000 people?" I asked, "There must have been an awful lot of dogs running around back then."

"Well sure, of course we did," Horace asserted, gaining control of himself, "I was just a youngster on the city council back then, but I remember we had a devil of a time controlling all those damn dogs, and we finally had to enact a dog by-law to get things under control."

"And did you ever repeal the by-law?" I asked.

"I guess not. When the city shrunk to the size of a town, and then a small town, I guess somewhere along the way we just stopped enforcing it," he said. "Why, are you planning to go out and arrest all the dogs in town?" he asked, starting to chuckle again.

"No, I have more than enough to do without looking for more work, thank you very much," I retorted, "Here's the thing. You know that Ruby inherited Silver, and has given him to me?"

He nodded. News travelled fast.

"Well, I'm going to want to be able to take Silver with me when I travel beyond Radium City. If I take him to, let's say Fort McMurray or Prince Albert, and we get separated, I might not be able to find him. If that happens, and if someone else finds him, then how will they know that he belongs to someone, or who to call? They might just put him down. But if he has a Radium City licence tag on him, then both questions are answered, and they'll call here first."

"I'm sorry Alex," Horace said, soberly. (We were on a first-name basis now. Finding a dead man together can do that.) "I see that you have thought this through, and that's actually a pretty good idea."

Horace searched through a series of old filing cabinets until finally, with an exclamation of success, he brought out a box containing dog licence forms, and licence tags with matching numbers. Filling out a form I passed it over to him and asked,

"How much?"

Scratching his head and looking at the register, he eventually said, "According to this we haven't issued a dog licence since 1962, ... and the last time the licence fee was raised was in, ... 1955!" he said, triumphantly.

"And," I prompted.

"And what?"

"And what does it cost now?"

"Oh, well, in 1955 we raised the licence fee to $5. Caused quite a stir, it did. Some of the people in town were quite incensed about it. Anyway, that means the fee is $5"

"Still?" I asked.

"Until the town council changes it, that's the fee," Horace said.

Now it was my turn to laugh. I paid the fee and went out to the sidewalk to show Silver his new licence. He sniffed at it and gave it a lick, but he didn't look very impressed.

I didn't have a collar for him, and I had a feeling that the general store owner's reaction to asking for a collar would lead to the same kind of vaudeville response I'd received from Horace. Instead, I went back to the detachment and rummaged through a couple of boxes of left-over clothes and other items that had been left behind by previous personnel. In the end, I was able to make a beautiful collar from an old Sam Browne[13] shoulder strap. With a little polish, the brown leather and brass buckle really shone, and the whole effect had an official RCMP look to it. Silver was fine with wearing the collar and licence tag, and I didn't push my luck by trying to get him on a leash.

Meanwhile, I had been thinking about dates. Not the romantic kind of dates, calendar dates: it was now Tuesday, September the 16th. If I was right that the Consolidated Bell Mines stock-purchase warrant existed, had been stolen by the murderer, and were the reason for the murderer's hurry, then according to Andrew at the bank the murderer would have to have someone physically deliver the certificates to a registered stockbroker's office before they expire on the 30th. Andrew recommended two business days before, to allow time for the broker to make all the arrangements, so that would move the deadline to September 28th. That would be a Sunday, so make it Friday the 26th.

So far so good. Now, either the certificates had already been exercised or they hadn't. Now that it was a murder investigation, I could ask Andrew to check with the closest brokers to see if anyone had brought them in already and to ask them to notify us if they surfaced in the next two weeks. Andrew had agreed to this and promised to alert the brokers in all the major cities between Alberta and Manitoba.

My work would involve assuming that they had not yet been exercised. That assumption meant that sometime in the next week and a half, someone was going to try to get the certificates out of Radium City. I was guessing that the murderer was unlikely to trust anyone else enough to handle the certificates, and would therefore make the trip in person. Even if I was wrong, if we could catch anyone in possession of the certificates we'd have another lead. Naturally, however, I hoped to catch the actual murderer directly.

The trouble now was, our murderer could go to any registered broker in any big city, not just the closest one, and we wouldn't be able to watch them all. Furthermore, having found Norm, everyone in town would now know about his death. Of course, I'd made Horace and Dr. Evans swear not to say anything about the manner of his death, or that we police considered it suspicious, but the murderer (or murderers) would know and would be on guard. Would they flee immediately, or lie low and try to avoid notice?

Our murderer would be wary, but so far there would be no reason for them to suspect that anyone knew what was stolen from Norm's house, nor about the way to make money from it.

I returned to the hospital and found Mike eager to discuss the case. I asked him how he would get out of Radium City if he was in a hurry.

"Until the lake freezes and a winter road is plowed, the only ways out are by boat or aircraft," he said, "You can go to Stony Rapids by boat and then drive to Winnipeg – that would take about 24 hours – or you could just fly commercial to Saskatoon and then connect onto a flight to Winnipeg. Depending on the flight connections, that would take about 3 hours to Saskatoon, then another 2 hours to Winnipeg – allowing, say, an hour between flights that would be something like 6 hours all told. Of course, there are only three scheduled flights per week: they fly in and out again every Monday, Wednesday, and Friday. The only other options would be to hire a charter aircraft in from, say Fort McMurray, or to get Vern to make the flight in his plane."

"That's it?"

"The only other way I can think of would be to go out on the barge. That would be chancy though, because it only comes in about once a week, not always on schedule, and when it leaves here it could just as easily be headed for any of the communities on the lake. Even to Waterways, Alberta, which is a very long trip from here."

"So what it comes down to is, to keep someone here we'd have to shut the airport down and prevent all boats from leaving, and hold everything up for ten days," I concluded.

"You're not serious!" Mike said, with eyes wide.

"Maybe not," I relented, "but I'd be tempted to try it if I could," and then, thinking furiously, "If we can't build a trap around our murderer, maybe we can get our murderer to step into a trap."

"What are you thinking?"

"I don't know yet, but I'll think of something. Maybe I'll go do some more research."

I went off to check the commercial flight and barge schedules for the next week and a half. The regular flights were still scheduled, but I got a break on the barge. It turned out that the barge was already out at Waterways, Alberta. It was apparently busy ferrying materials from the railhead up to Fort McMurray for a new oil sands mine, called Syncrude, that was under construction. It would be busy over there for at least the next two weeks. Then, I went to see Vern and his plane.

Vern wasn't at the airport, but the commercial air service people suggested I try the marina. I hadn't received the impression that Vern was interested in boats but dutifully followed up, and sure enough, Vern was there, and so was his plane. He explained that he'd shifted from conventional landing wheels to floats so that he'd be able to do some fly-in fishing with some friends that would be coming up to visit the following month. Vern explained that he'd put the floats on early so he could go and scout a couple of new fishing lakes he'd heard about from Jim and Horace. I'd brought a thermos of coffee with me in the police truck and offered him a cup in return for answering some more questions I had about flying in the north.

The next day was Wednesday, and I just 'happened' to be at the airport around noon, when the scheduled flight from Saskatoon and Prince Albert came. It had a load of people coming in, but just a couple of teenagers flying out. So far, so good.

Later that afternoon, I dropped into Ruby's café, partly to see how she was bearing up under her grief and partly just to grab a cup of tea and visit.

"Did you hear about the airport?" Ruby asked.

"The airport?"

"Yeah, the airport's going to be closed for a week. Maybe two weeks!"

"Really, what for?" I asked.

"Some kind of work on the runway marker lights. Some federal aviation authority people of some kind are coming up to replace them. They're coming over by boat from Fond-du-Lac with the new lights. Should be here tomorrow or Friday."

I saw that Vern was sitting with Ron (and Ally) and Jim over cups of coffee, in a booth nearby, and called over to him. "Hey, Vern, what's up with the runway?"

"They're finally going to do the lighting upgrades we've been bugging them for," said Vern. "You know those white lights that run along on both sides of the runway?"

I nodded.

"Well, in good visibility conditions those lights are white. In poor visibility conditions, when pilots are flying on instruments only, what we call IFR. The white lights change to yellow when the aircraft gets to the last half of the runway, and then they turn red when the aircraft gets to the end of the runway ... kind of important when the visibility's low. You don't want to run off the sides or the end of the runway!"

"Right, ..."

"Anyway," Vern continued, "The runway lights we have are really old and the technology has improved a lot. We're finally getting an upgrade to HIRL, which stands for 'high-intensity runway lighting.' This is going to make life easier, and safer, for all pilots flying in and out, especially when the winter comes and we have short days and lots of snowstorms."

Ruby chimed in, "The only problem is getting supplies over the next two weeks, but Vern has offered to help out. See," she said, pointing to a typed sheet of paper thumbtacked to her community noticeboard.

I went over and read:

> **NOTICE:**
>
> If anyone has an urgent need for anything over the next two weeks, while our airport is being upgraded, I'm going to be flying south twice and am willing to pick-up things, within reason, and fly them up to Radium City.
>
> My two scheduled trips are:
>
> 1. Friday, Sept. 19, 11 am, to Prince Albert,
> 2. Tuesday, Sept. 30, 11 am, to Fort McMurray.
>
> Vern Schriver

"That's very nice of you Vern. I'm sure people will really appreciate it," I said. "As a matter of fact, I have a small package that I need to send down, would you be willing to take it for me? I can get someone from the Prince Albert detachment to come to the airport to meet you and pick it up."

"Sure Alex, I'd be glad to."

"Do you have other errands to run?"

"Well, I have a fairly long list of small things. I only put the list up a couple of hours ago and it seems like everyone in town knows about it already."

"Sounds great. I'll see you on Friday then, with my package."

Vern simply gave a distracted wave and went back to his coffee. I visited with Ruby a little longer and then headed back to the detachment to catch up on some paperwork.

It was a long wait until Friday, and I was waiting 'on pins and needles' the whole time, but the day and a half eventually did pass.

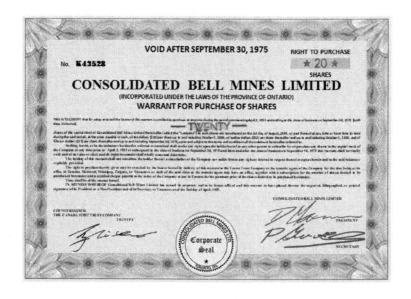

15 "COME INTO MY PARLOUR"

On Friday morning, Silver and I drove to the marina with my package for Prince Albert. I didn't have a specific plan for Silver, but I had taken the precaution of removing his new collar, not wanting to advertise that he'd become anything other than "Norm's dog."

Vern's plane was tied-up at the same pier where I had seen it earlier in the week and he was pulling seats out again, presumably to make room for the parcels he'd be bringing back from Prince Albert.

"Got any passengers coming with you?" I asked, as nonchalantly as I could.

"Not so far, but you never know. Someone may just show up at the last minute," he replied.

These words were no sooner out of his mouth than we heard the sound of a vehicle approaching and Ron's old truck appeared over the crest of the hill, on its way down to us at the marina.

Hmmm, I thought.

Ron asked if he could catch a ride with Vern, who agreed, and the three of us just stood around waiting in silence, each lost in their own thoughts. For my part, I was still having trouble visualizing Ron as our murderer, but by showing up when he did I was forced to raise him up higher on my mental suspect list.

We waited and waited, but by 11 am, no one else had come. Vern was just saying, "Maybe we should wait a few more minutes and see if …" when two vehicles came down the gravel road to the marina. One was Dr. Evans' bright red Suburban SUV, and the other was an older pickup truck that I didn't recognize right away. They both parked, and then Dr. Evans and Jim got out of their vehicles and walked down to the docks together, the former carrying a cardboard box, and the latter with a shoulder bag slung from one shoulder.

Dr. Evans asked Vern if he had room for one more box.

"You bet," said Vern, "most people want me to pick-up stuff, so I'm pretty much flying down empty."

"Does that mean you have room for a passenger then?" Jim asked.

"Sure thing Jim," Vern said, and then, looking at him shrewdly, "no charge."

I was so surprised that Jim also wanted to fly out, that I hesitated for a moment as a whole bunch of things clicked together in my mind. Ron was strong, but he wasn't big enough to have been the person that had attacked me in the bookstore. But Jim, ... Instinctively, without conscious thought I found myself taking a step forward and blurting out "Jim! It was you that attacked me in the bookstore that night!"

At this, Jim immediately turned white as a sheet and involuntarily backed-up a step. "Now wait a minute, who says I was ever there?" he began, but the rest of his words were lost as Silver started barking and advancing towards him. In response, Jim backed up another step and started looking around as if trying to decide whether or not to bolt and run.

Meanwhile, Silver continued to advance slowly, barking furiously, to the point of getting his whole shoulders into the movement of his barks. I'd never seen him do that before, and it was clearly enough to frighten Jim, who had slipped his satchel off his shoulder and turned as if to run back up the dock.

Before he'd taken two more steps, Silver lunged forward, grabbed the satchel strap in his jaws and pulled it away from Jim. Then it was Silver that ran to the end of the dock, followed by Jim and the rest of us.

Silver had stopped when he reached the shore and was growling and shaking his head furiously, still with the satchel in his mouth, as if he'd caught a rabbit or something and was trying to snap its neck by violently shaking it back and forth.

Jim seemed to have gotten over his momentary fear of Silver, as he was yelling at him to let go. As he reached Silver, he grabbed the satchel strap too. In the few moments that it took the rest of us to catch up, Jim and Silver had engaged in a violent tug of war, with Jim yelling and Silver growling as they struggled over the satchel. Just as we caught up to them, the strap tore away from the satchel, causing Jim to fall back, holding one piece. Silver, being better balanced on four legs was just standing there with another piece hanging out of his jaws. In between them flew a cloud of the papers that had been in the satchel.

As Jim started crawling toward the papers, trying to gather them all up in his arms, Dr. Evans, Vern, Ron, and I each grabbed a few ourselves.

I glanced at the top piece of paper that I had picked up, and read the bold type at its top: "Consolidated Bell Mines Limited," and in smaller type: "Warrant for Purchase of Shares."

"Well Jim, I guess we know what was stolen from Norm's place now don't we?"

As I advanced toward him, he said, "Those are mine. You don't have anything on me," and as I continued to advance, "You wouldn't arrest a friend, would you?"

"Jim, we've been friends, and I'll grant that you might not have known it was me in the bookstore - maybe you just panicked - but the break-ins were no accident. Norm is dead, and that might have been an accident too, although you should have at least reported it and not just left him out there in a cold mine shaft. Anyway, you'll get your chance to tell it all to a judge. For now, my duty comes first and you have to be held to account for your actions."

Saying this, I'd come up close enough to Jim to put my hand on his shoulder and say, as I'd been taught, "James Dumont, I arrest you for the murder of Norman Poole. You need not say anything. You have nothing to hope from any promise or favour, and nothing to fear from any threat, whether or not you say anything. Anything you do or say may be used as evidence against you at your trial."

I handcuffed Jim, led him to our police truck, and seated him in the back, while he muttered darkly about 'damn Mounties and their damn dogs.'

As I did this, Dr. Evans had gone up to his SUV, taken a wheelchair out of the back and helped Mike into it. Mike had been sitting inside, quietly observing the whole incident. Ron had whistled long and low when he'd read the text printed on the stock purchase warrants, and he explained to the others that anyone could take them to a broker and use them to buy the actual stock – cheap! I could tell from his tone of surprise that he'd been completely unaware of their existence until now.

For myself, on top of everything else, I was amazed to see Mike out of the hospital.

When I asked how Mike had managed to get released early, they explained that Mike had been adamant that he "wasn't going to sit cooped-up in bed and miss this." Conversely, Dr. Evans had been just as adamant that Mike wasn't ready to go "roaming around town" yet. They had compromised on Mike agreeing to both using the wheelchair and having Dr. Evans come along to make sure he didn't overdo it.

At this point, we heard the sound of an approaching aircraft, and we all looked up to see the regular commercial flight from Prince Albert fly over us *en route* to the airport.

"What the Hell??" exclaimed Dr. Evans, "I thought the airport was closed for two weeks!"

"So did everyone," Mike said, grinning, "especially Jim over there."

Jim could be heard all the way from the back of our police truck swearing loudly and sulfurously.

"It was all a trick," Mike explained, exhibiting his Cheshire Cat smile. "Alex here wanted to get the airport shut down. She couldn't manage that, so she did the next best thing and made everyone except Vern here think that it was shut down."

"I had thought of watching the airport and the air service bookings," I explained, "but then I would have had to watch all the boats as well, which would have been too much."

"I got a lucky break with the barge being away, and no one else but Vern had a private plane in town. Even so, I still had to deal with the commercial air service and the boats. So, I got Vern here to help me create the illusion of the airport shutting down, and set-up Vern and his plane as an easy opportunity to quickly get to Prince Albert. From there, it would have been easy to connect to flights to Winnipeg. Our murderer could still have snuck out by boat, but I hoped he take the easier and faster opportunity, especially since Vern would probably have taken him for free!"

"Very smart, and very convincing," Dr. Evans offered, "You

certainly had me fooled."

"Me too," offered Ron, scratching his head as he put all the pieces together in his mind.

"I had more than just Mike and Vern's help," I added. "Silver was really the one that prevented Jim from getting away."

"It was a good thing he grabbed at the satchel and, by fighting over it, got it torn-up enough that the certificates fell out," Mike added. "Otherwise, we'd have had to do a lot of fast talking to try to get a search warrant for it, and by then Jim might have simply denied everything and gotten away."

"Yes, he leaped forward at Jim as soon as I accused him of jumping me in the bookstore. I don't know what made him decide to do that, whether it was my tone of voice, or Jim turning pale and looking guilty, or if he somehow knew it had been Jim all along."

"That's a very unusual dog," Mike concluded, not for the first time.

"I was lucky that Jim went for the 'bait,' and I was lucky to have Silver jump in at just the right time," I said, reattaching Silver's fancy leather collar.

"Nonsense," Mike jumped in, "A Mountie doesn't rely on luck!"

Wait for it, I thought to myself, *here comes Mike the professor.*

"A Mountie, plans ahead, is resourceful, is tenacious, ... and you know what they say ..." he paused for effect.

We all looked at him expectantly, as he put on his professorial look and proclaimed:

"A Mountie always gets **her** man!"

James Dumont

16 EPILOGUE

I was able to call a Magistrate in Prince Albert and submit my application for a warrant by telephone. Two hours later, we received a printed search warrant by telex.

My search of Jim's house turned up a small library of materials that were consistent with, but different from, the mine histories, prospecting stories, maps, and journals that had been sifted through in the bookstore, and the government geological reports that had been sifted through in the library. All told, it made for a pretty comprehensive looking collection.

The most telling find, however, was a complete looking set of calculations, among which featured estimates of the gold potential in a wide range of former uranium mines of the area, together with estimates of the dollar value of the gold that could potentially be realized from each of the mines. Looking at Jim's list of final estimates, it was clear that the gold potential of most of the old uranium mines was quite low, except for two mines: The Bell-A and the Bell-B mines!

We had confiscated the stock purchase warrants from Jim's satchel of course. There were lots of them. The warrants were for different numbers of shares, but otherwise, the wording, numbers, and dates were identical.

Here is an example of what the warrants said:

> THIS IS TO CERTIFY that for value received the bearer of this warrant is entitled to purchase at any time during the period commencing April 2, 1955, and ending at the close of business on September 30, 1975 (both days inclusive): TWENTY shares of the capital stock of Consolidated Bell Mines Limited (hereinafter called the "Company") as such shares are constituted on the 1st day of August, 1954, or part thereof at any time or from time to time during the said period, at the price payable in cash, of ten dollars ($10) per share up to and including October 1, 1965; of twelve dollars ($12) per share thereafter and up to and including October 1, 1970; and of fifteen dollars ($15) per share thereafter and up to and including September 30, 1975, upon and subject to the terms and conditions of the indenture hereinafter referred to.
>
> Nothing herein, or in the indenture hereinafter referred to contained shall confer any right upon the holder hereof or any other person to subscribe for or purchase any shares in the capital stock of the Company at any time prior to April 2, 1955 or subsequent to the close of business on September 30, 1975 and from and after the close of business on September 30, 1975 this warrant shall be wholly void and of no value or effect and all rights hereunder shall wholly cease and determine.

So, there we had it, *"and from and after the close of business on September 30, 1975, this warrant shall be wholly void and of no value or effect and all rights hereunder shall wholly cease and determine."* That set the deadline, just as Andrew had predicted. So now we knew for sure.

I read on:

> The right to purchase hereby given may be exercised by the bearer hereof by delivery of this warrant to the Crown Trust Company or the transfer agent of the Company for the time being at its office in Toronto, Montreal, Winnipeg, Calgary, or Vancouver or such of the said cities as the transfer agent may have an office, together with a subscription for the number of shares desired to be purchased hereunder and a certified cheque payable to the order of the Company at par in Toronto for the purchase price of the shares desired to be purchased hereunder.

That fixed the place, *"... may be exercised by the bearer hereof by delivery of this warrant to the Crown Trust Company or the transfer agent of the Company for the time being at its office in Toronto, Montreal, Winnipeg, Calgary, or Vancouver ..."* The nearest such office was in Winnipeg.

I'd taken the stock purchase warrants over to show Andrew at the bank. We'd found ninety altogether, fifty for the purchase of twenty shares each, twenty for the purchase of fifty shares each, and thirty for the purchase of one hundred shares each.

"Norm's father must have really believed in the potential of the Bell mines," Andrew concluded, "He probably bought shares in the company when he worked there. Any time the company put new shares out on the market, they would have offered these share purchase warrants as an inducement for people to buy the stock. At the time, the company probably offered something like one or maybe two future share purchases for each actual share purchased. So, if Norm's father bought, say a hundred shares, then he'd get warrants enabling him to purchase another hundred or two hundred at a future date, for the prices we saw listed on the warrants."

"Why so many certificates then?"

"He probably bought different numbers of shares from time to time. Some combination of when they were made available and when he could afford them. Then again, I suppose the company might have given him some warrants directly as a kind of bonus or extra pay. I suspect another thing that happened, though, is that he probably had bought a lot of these warrants from other investors as they lost confidence in the operation over the years."

"How do the numbers add up?" I asked.

"Well, all together these warrants can be used to buy five thousand shares at fifteen dollars a share. If they're used before they expire, then that would cost $75,000, plus a small brokerage fee. In 1970, the shares were trading for twelve dollars a share. At that time, these warrants were completely worthless, but since then the stock price has more than tripled, to thirty-eight dollars a share. So, at the current price, you'd be paying $75,000 for $190,000 worth of shares."

I whistled sharply, "That's not bad, you'd more than double your money. I wonder whether Norm was planning to use them himself. I guess we'll never know."

"Wait, it gets better," Andrew exclaimed. "Let's say someone buys the shares like we just said, and then waits for the news to get out about the gold potential of the mines. That would drive the share price even higher. I could see it easily doubling, or more. If it doubles, then you could sell the shares while the market for them is hot and turn your $75,000 into at least $380,000! Think of what you could do with that kind of money, that's enough …"

"To kill for, … yes," I interjected, dampening Andrew's excitement at the numbers.

"Could you take control of the company with those shares?" I asked.

"Probably not. We're talking about five thousand shares here, and my broker says that there are something like a million shares outstanding. But, simply selling them would make someone a lot of money if the mine was reopened and put into production for the gold."

"Well, I guess that will be up to Ruby. We'll have to get some legal advice on how we can preserve the evidence value of the warrants and still let Ruby exercise them before the expiry date, if she wants to," I mused, "I'll let her know what we've figured out so far and suggest that she talk to Frank about it and get his advice."

In training, we'd been taught that peoples' appearances can be deceiving — hardly a stunning revelation - but one that can be difficult to always bear in mind. If I'd needed an object lesson, then it was provided by Norm, and Ron, and Jim. Norm's aggressive and surly manner hid a willingness to help people, and a deep respect for people and nature. Ron's lack of interest in other people made him seem almost rude, and certainly suspicious. Although Jim's preoccupation with money was impossible to miss, his outgoing, friendly, and perennially happy demeanour hid a selfish and ruthless nature. I found that sad.

I've mentioned Jim's love of talking and story-telling. Although I'd warned him about the hazards of saying anything that might be incriminating, after a day in jail he became quite talkative. I'd expected him to continue to plead innocence, but once he started talking the story tumbled out, and he surprised me by confessing to the whole thing.

It was in a casual conversation with Norm that Jim had learned about the gold potential. He hadn't let on to Norm but had secretly done his own planning and research, hoping to maximize the potential payout he could get.

He said that he hadn't planned to kill Norm. He was going to keep everything secret, and simply steal the stock purchase warrants from him. In his own mind, he had rationalized that Norm would still come out of it all ahead of the game because Norm had a lot of actual shares of the company registered in his own name (the ones he'd inherited from his father). The trap in the abandoned mine raise wasn't intended to kill, he insisted, it was to put a big scare into anyone that got interested in the mine and his idea was that it would persuade them to stay away.

It turned out that Norm had gone to look around the Bell-A mine on Bell Island, and Jim said he'd only noticed it by accident. Jim had apparently been headed for a completely different destination that day and had seen Norm's boat pulled-up on Bell Island. Jim had pulled in alongside and gone to see what Norm was up to. Discovering that his trap hadn't worked, Jim had lured Norm (but not Silver) over to the Bell-B mine. In the process, Norm told Jim his ideas about the mineral value left in the two Bell mines, and that he thought there might be enough gold to justify reopening one or both mines. Jim hadn't been too worried at first and had simply pretended ignorant interest. When Norm said that he was planning to bring in a drilling rig to get new samples and have them assayed, Jim panicked, grabbed a large rock when Norm's back was turned, and killed him. He'd then dragged Norm's body into the side passage where Horace and I had found it and left it there thinking that he'd be able to get back and move the body to a better hiding place long before anyone else happened along.

Jim had later gone back to Bell Island, retrieved Norm's boat (once again abandoning Silver to the island), and towed it back to Radium City, timing the journey so that he'd reach the marina at about 3 am, so he could tie-up Norm's boat in its usual berth without much chance of being spotted.

Andrew and I had been right about the financial aspects. Jim admitted that he had just over $75,000 as his life savings. He was planning to simply buy some shares on the market, but then he'd realized that he could make a lot more money if he could get the warrants and use them before word got out about the gold, and before they expired. His big hurry, of course, had been because of the expiry date.

Jim's estimate of the future share value was higher than ours though. He figured that once news of the gold potential became public, that the stock would rise by another 250%, in which case he'd have been able to fairly quickly turn his $75,000 investment into $475,000. With nearly half a million dollars he was going to move south and retire to a "life of ease."

17 LOOSE ENDS

So, that was my first experience with small-town policing.
    I'd gotten what I'd asked for, and more. I got my chance to try "real policing." I'd had to face new challenges, and I'd learned a lot. Along the way, a few things had happened that scared the hell out of me, but I'd survived them. In a bizarre set of crises, I'd been able to rescue Mike from one mine floor collapse and then had a strange dog named Silver rescue me from another – and gained two new friends in the process. Looking back, I realized that I'd grown up a bit too.
    Four months! It had all happened in four months.
    In comparison, the months of October and November were pretty quiet. Mike was allowed out of the hospital, on crutches, a few days after I'd arrested Jim, and it didn't take long for him to get his strength back and leave the crutches behind. That allowed us to ease back into a more sustainable routine. We'd now learned the value of having Jennifer cover the daytime phone and telex, and few other tasks for us. She was still undecided about her long-term future and had loved working with us, so we found a way to keep her on, out of our meagre detachment maintenance budget.
    Winter comes early in the North, and we had snow on the ground by mid-October, and a thick snow cover by Halloween.
    Halloween! I was remembering Norm and his snarky question about Halloween when I'd landed in Radium City for the very first time when we received an unusual telex. It rather cryptically informed us that Assistant Commissioner MacLeod was going to

be flying by police plane the following day, and would make a brief stopover in Radium City. "Unofficial visit. No ceremony," it said.

"Something's up," I said.

"Know him?" asked Mike.

"We've met. He's the one that talked me into leaving Metro Toronto to join the Force."

"Mmmmm. Something tells me you're getting transferred."

"What, already? I've only been here six months!"

Mike steepled his fingers and shifted into professorial mode. "True, but sometimes summer replacements are just that – summer replacements."

"I guess," I said, thinking about it. Mike interrupted my thoughts:

"Speaking of telexes, I saw the telex you sent about my mine accident. Very concise, to the point, and factual. A model telex … In fact, if a person reading that telex didn't know better, they'd be forced to conclude that the ground simply collapsed under my weight. The kind of thing that could have happened to anyone …"

"Well, that's true," I offered.

"What you probably should have added, was that it was caused by my own bloody idiotic, schoolboy theatrics!" he said, having shifted to his gruff expression and peering at me from between his bushy eyebrows and his thick handlebar moustache.

"Maybe," I said, "but there was no harm done, other than to yourself, and I thought that you were going to pay a pretty stiff price already, what with being confined to traction for so long, without having to have it on your record as well."

His face softened at this point, and he dialled his voice down from parade ground to bedside, "Thanks, Alex."

"None needed … but you're welcome."

The next day, Mike and I were both at the airport to greet Assistant Commissioner MacLeod, who disembarked from the police plane in civilian clothes – a plain suit that wouldn't be out of place in any big corporation, anywhere. Following a quick drive around town and coffee with both of us back at the detachment, he eventually shifted to a change in body language that Mike correctly interpreted as a polite signal for him to leave us.

When it was just the two of us, he asked how I now felt about having joined the RCMP, and about my experiences in Radium City. These were clearly more than casual questions, as he quite thoroughly questioned me about specific aspects of my experiences, how I'd handled them, and how I felt about them with the clarity of hindsight. I was surprised to find that he seemed to be as interested in my approaches to policing, and getting to know the area and its people as he was about our murder-robbery case. He also seemed to have already been aware of the Silver connection and had a lot of questions about him too.

After a thorough debriefing, it wouldn't have taken a genius to detect that I was wondering what all this was about, and this was clearly a very intelligent man. He knew what I was thinking, and he also saved me from trying to figure out how to go about interrogating such a senior officer, by smoothly moving the topic of conversation forward.

He explained that earlier in the year he had been transferred from 'Depot' Division to become the new head of the Security Service[14]. He added that, although things there were in pretty good shape, he had some new ideas he wanted to try out, and just like when he was at 'Depot' Division, he intended to launch a few experimental pilot projects.

"Like me?" I asked.

"Exactly," he said, "Although a lot of my experiments don't work out as planned, ..." He paused, as if in thought for a moment, and then he beamed: "But this one did! You have proven yourself royally. I'd have been happy if you'd done half as well as you have. Following in your bootsteps," he chuckled as his own joke, "the first full troop of women is in training in 'Depot' Division right now, and by next Spring, they'll be getting posted right across the country."

"That's great," I said, "So you don't need me anymore?"

"Hardly," he said sharply, "We have another opportunity now. Most people won't be used to the idea of a woman Mountie for a few years yet. I think there might be a few ways we can use that to our advantage, don't you? ... I want you to come and work for me."

"What about Cpl. Morrison, Sir? Shouldn't I stay on here and help him get fully up to speed again first?"

"Cpl. Morrison is as strong as a horse," he replied. "He's back on his feet, and the truth is, he can run this detachment single-handed. That's partly why I got you assigned here in the first place, so you'd have a chance to show what you could do without having been 'set-up to fail' – and it worked beyond anything any of us could have imagined! Besides, he'll be getting a replacement for you anyway."

Before I could respond to this, he continued, "I've already spoken to him about this, but I ordered him not to tell you until I could get here in person. You should know that he fought hard to keep you. I'd worried about sending you to work with such an old traditionalist and hard-liner, but you obviously proved yourself with him, and that's another point in your favour."

I smiled, "His bark was a lot worse than his bite, sir, and I found gold under that crusty, traditionalist outer layer of his. In the end, honour and common sense won out over his prejudices and preconceived notions."

"May that be said of any of us," said the Assistant Commissioner.

Then, as if sensing that the conversation was turning slightly soapy, he pulled himself together with a gruff "Harumph," that would have impressed even Sergeant Major Walsh. "In any case, you've already learned most of what there is to learn in Radium City. It's time to transfer you on to something new, and as I said, I'd like you to come work for me. I could just arrange to have you transferred, but I want you to come willingly, and I'll want you to be totally committed."

And then, just like he'd said over a year previously, in Toronto: "Will you do it?"

Before I could answer, he added, "You'd better bring that dog of yours too. I have a feeling you wouldn't leave without him, and we might just need him. What do you say?"

The man was a mind-reader! All I could do was say "Yes, Sir!"

***

... Alex and Silver will return, in "*An Inconspicuous Mountie.*"

Laurie Schramm

ABOUT THE AUTHOR

Laurie Schramm comes from an RCMP family, grew up while living in the RCMP Barracks ('Depot' Division) in Regina, Saskatchewan, and spent several summers working as a civilian for the RCMP while in high school and university. Early personal influences included not only the real-life RCMP culture but also Hollywood's versions via such classics as *Rose Marie,* and *Susannah of the Mounties*. Many of the events described in this novel are based on the author's real life, although not necessarily within an RCMP context.

For more information, see Laurier L. Schramm on **Linked in**.

ENDNOTES

1. In real life, a first full troop of women began training in the RCMP in 1974, but for this fictional story, it all began with a single-woman pilot test.
2. These movies can be found on the internet.
3. Physical training, outdoors or in the gym.
4. Like a troop leader, but without any real authority. The Right Marker deals with roll call, marching the troop here and there, and serving as a liaison for administrative matters affecting the troop.
5. Equitation was dropped from recruit training in 1965, but for this story, I left it in for another decade.
6. Non-commissioned officer in charge.
7. The telex network was a switched network of teleprinters similar to a telephone network, that enabled text-based messages to be sent and received. It had evolved from the old telegraph systems.
8. Within the RCMP are distinguished "Members," or "Regular Members," meaning official police officers of any rank, and "Civilian Members," meaning non-officer employees.
9. However, of the "open files," a smaller number would actually be considered "active" at any given time.
10. It did eventually become a protected area, as the Athabasca Sand Dunes Provincial Wilderness Park, but not until 1992.
11. A piece of metal looking vaguely like the number eight, but with one end larger than the other. When threaded with a climbing rope this device creates enough friction to enable a climber to control their rate of descent with a single hand while rappelling.

12. Which it did, in 1979.
13. A Sam Browne belt is a wide leather belt, supported by a narrow leather strap passing diagonally over the (usually) right shoulder. Captain Sam Browne VC, who lost his left arm in combat in India in 1858, needed a way to hold his scabbard in place so he could draw his sword one-handed. He invented this belt, which had hooks for attaching the scabbard on the left side, while the diagonal strap was used to support its weight. His pistol was carried in a flap-style holster on the right side. The RCMP version is made of brown leather.
14. At this point in time it was still part of the RCMP, but in 1984 the Security Service was spun-out to create the present-day Canadian Security Intelligence Service (CSIS).

ADVENTURES OF THE FIRST WOMAN MOUNTIE

Book 1: *An Inconvenient Mountie*
Book 2: *An Inconspicuous Mountie*
Book 3: *An Indestructible Mountie*
Book 4: *An International Mountie*
Book 5: *An Inseparable Mountie*

Laurie Schramm

Made in the USA
Lexington, KY
05 December 2018